# 50 SHADES OF WORF

by

Christopher D. Schmitz

Right' in the dragonballs!

PUBLISHED BY TREESHAKER BOOKS
please visit:
http://www.authorchristopherdschmitz.com

# 50 Shades of Worf

## by

## Christopher D. Schmitz

Please note:
This is a work of fiction. Even though this story uses the names of several real-life figures from pop-culture, each instance is entirely made up. No disrespect is intended and they are used entirely as homage to each person's contribution to popular culture as a whole.

This story employs parody and satire and no harm (to person or reputation) is intended towards any person involved. I use a few famous people sparingly in my plot and for humorous purposes. If a setting or scene makes you think poorly of that person, remember that these settings are not true. These situations are only used in a manner consistent with parody.

# Special Offer:

Get a free 5-book Starter Library from Christopher
Schmitz FOR FREE
Details found at the end of this book. Subscribers who
sign up for this no-spam newsletter get free books,
exclusive content, and more!

# Dedication

I'd like to dedicate this book to the drunk lady I once met on the light rail. We bonded over Taco Bell and bodily functions. You were too hammered to remember our conversation (either time we had it), but may this book give you some reading (and emergency paper) for your next post-taco experience.

# PART ONE

## SMILE

# 1

Pollando

Moses Farnsworth pulled his eyes away from the out-dated computer monitor and looked up from his desk at the precinct office. The lines of his crisp, blue uniform slouched and bent over the curves of his slightly overweight body. At least the poorly fitting class Bs helped draw attention away from the greasy food stains that mottled his periwinkle canvas.

He peered over his desk's crowded collection of action figures and repositioned the few that fellow officers had gesticulated into inappropriate poses. Beyond the line of fictitious, plastic heroes stood Farnsworth's real ones.

Farnsworth tensed and sat a little taller as the homicide detectives walked nearer. Rick Diego was a mountain of a man who Farnsworth guessed could've made a killing in the professional wrestling scene if he'd had any inclination, and barely nodded to the starry-eyed policeman. Diego's partner, Jared McCloud winked at Farnsworth and pointed at the figures with his fistful of coffee.

"I see you got a new addition," he commented as he passed with a wink. "I'm digging the sorcerer."

Diego rolled his eyes as they passed. They headed for their Captain's office.

Barely raising his voice as they walked by, Farnsworth commented too late, "It's a prototype Pollando the Blue Wizard

I got as a Kickfunder backer bonus." He didn't think anyone heard him.

"Don't encourage him," Diego said to McCloud, just loud enough for Farnsworth to hear.

"C'mon, man. I've never seen an officer as good as him with kids. Mark my words—he'll make detective someday."

The two took a seat near the Captain's office door and waited for her to arrive. McCloud's words hung in the air and tugged the edges of Farnsworth's lips into a smile. He hadn't had a win in a few days... at least not outside the local Magic the Gathering tournament at the nearest comic book shop, but the Goblin Hole didn't count.

Glancing down into the waste bin nearest his desk, Farnsworth spotted his application to take the Detective's Exam. He reached down and fished out the wrinkled mess. As he laid it back onto his desk, he reconsidered trying it again. He would have to get it signed and submitted by lunch. The test was scheduled for that weekend.

He bit his lip; it's all he'd ever really wanted. An officer could take it as many times as necessary to pass, but he could only take it so many times before his pride would quit on him. He knew he was the laughing stock of his peers... but he *did* have *some* pride.

With a metal on metal screech, the officer pulled open his desk drawer and spotted a thick fiction novel. Farnsworth retrieved his copy of the tome, *Knights of the Illuvian Age* by the late, great Sharyn J.R.R.K. McCrumb. He used its weighty mass to smooth out the crumpled paperwork. He'd almost gotten the kinks out of the forms when he heard something like a storm explode behind him.

Captain Lacey Murphy always moved like a whirlwind. The diminutive black woman's approach sent a shiver of dread rippling down Farnsworth's spine as she strode across the precinct floor.

In one fell, terrified sweep Farnsworth scooped the book and most of his action figures into the opened drawer. Just in time for her to see his screen he managed to click the minimize button on his web browser and hide the *Knights of the Illuvian Age* web forum where he'd been arguing casting choices for a potential, future movie incarnation.

His heart burst inside his ribcage as she walked past with all the grace of an Imperial AT-ST on the backwoods trails of Endor. Farnsworth cowered like an ewok and refused to make eye contact. His cup of water shivered with ripples from her frightening footsteps. *Don't move. Don't move... she can't see me if I don't move.*

She moved away from his section and slipped into her office with the homicide detectives in tow.

Finally looking up, he spotted Jennifer Quast flitting from desk to desk with a packet of info. She walked with her odd, signature gait, arms remaining still and motionless as she moved. The department had recently upgraded her to the role of Crime Analyst. He stared off into space, imagining her analyzing *him*.

Farnsworth tumbled from his reverie when she stood before him and put a print-out into his hand. The data sheet indicated that the notorious mafia hit man Gage Houdek was known to be back in town. The man the Russian mob called Zmei... the Dragon.

He scanned the info. They still hadn't gotten anything beyond a very generic description of him. He'd never been photographed. "Crap," he murmured, hoping that it wouldn't mean extra work. As the low man on the totem pole, even after years at the precinct, he usually got the garbage jobs.

# 2

## A 'Little' Drug Deal

Captain Murphy unscrewed the top of her thermos and poured a thick, sludgy stream of black coffee into her mug. Morning had barely arrived and she typically refused to say a word before slugging down at least half a cup of joe. At least, not any words appropriate for public. The Captain slid a manila folder across the table in silence.

McCloud picked it up and fanned the documents as he leafed through it. He knew better than to talk before she'd set the container down. There'd been one murder *already* today, and without him or his partner, there would be no one to investigate their own untimely demises if they poked the beast.

Murphy set her cup down and leaned back as her homicide detectives perused the briefly sketched data and dossiers. Satisfied by the caffeinated offering, the distance between her eyebrows spread ever so slightly and signaled it was safe to talk.

"Down by the docks," Diego noted. "Pretty cliche, if you ask me. Why doesn't anyone ever commit murder in places we'd want to go... like a nice steakhouse or a pro football game."

"He meant petting zoo," McCloud interjected.

She waved her hands and dismissed them. "Take him to the petting zoo or whatever. I don't care, just do your thing and find the..."

"Diego really could use a hug," McCloud slipped in.

"...just get this thing solved and in a hurry. Chief Cooper is breathing down my neck. I guess there's some kind of big, local event coming up in week or so and he wants the city to look its absolute finest. Part of the mayor's tourism initiative."

"What event?" Diego asked.

"Some nerd fest called TrollCON."

The two looked at each other confusedly and shrugged.

"It's a comic book convention," she clarified on the verge of shuddering.

"I think I have a weird nephew who is into stuff like that," Diego commented. "You know Dragons and Dungeons or whatever."

She continued unabated, "He's afraid of the drug element's presence on the street, as if thirty thousand adults in tights isn't scary enough. Let's not get them high and believing they can fly off roofs or whatever. Officer Quast said that there appears to have been 'a little drug deal' going down during last night's murder." Captain Murphy used air quotes to punctuate the quote.

The detectives traded glances. Neither knew how to understand the quote. Quast wasn't prone to bouts of great inflection when she spoke.

"Was that sarcasm, or what do you mean by 'a little drug deal?'" Diego asked. "Quast doesn't exactly have a way with words." He flipped through the envelope's contents and glanced at a sticky note where she'd drawn a doodle, as she often did. A junky made a snowman out of cocaine in the cartoon. *But she's got a way with art.*

Their boss fixed them with a hard look and slammed back the rest of her first cup. "How the heck should I know? You're the detectives." She made a shooing motion. "Now go detect things!"

# 3

Gotcha

McCloud and Diego walked past a row of neatly parked box-vans in the nearby lot. The vehicles' sun-faded decals read Union Industries in the same kitchie script as the building signage. Both Detectives had read the Captain's notes and were well aware that Union Industries was a shell company for the Russian mob.

They ducked under the crime scene tape and walked into the warehouse that overlooked the shipping docks. The dilapidated building had fallen to both the decay of time and the moral decline of the neighboring environment.

Several officers meandered about the scene cataloging and photographing details. Their footsteps crunched upon the cracked and busted concrete.

"What have we got here?" Diego barked the words as he stood over the trio of bodies that had crumpled where they'd fallen dead. A set of black, vulcanized rubber patches seemed to indicate a getaway driver had done a burnout leading away from the corpses.

McCloud walked away, following a blood trail as a uniformed officer handed a sheaf of notes to Diego. She pointed to each body in order. "Bullet to the face on him. Each of these ones took it to the side of the head."

Diego bit his lip and looked around the scene. He nodded to internally confirm his suspicions. "Must've been an inside job... I think these guys knew the shooter."

He looked towards his partner and then traced the blood trail back to a crimson pool that had gelled black near a derelict forklift. Diego walked to the silent machine where it rested near a huge bank of draped tarps. "What have you got, Jared?"

Detective McCloud crouched over a body lying face-down in the center of the warehouse a hundred feet away. "Two heel marks with the blood trail. He died over *there* and someone dragged him over *here*."

"Heel marks... face down? They took the extra effort to turn him over after the long drag?" Diego hollered over his shoulder. He peeled back the tarps and whistled. Five industrial pallets, each piled seven feet tall with bagged cocaine, hid beneath the tarps. "A *little* drug deal? Dang it, Quast," he muttered

Detective Diego traced his fingers in the dust near the forklift and then back at the skid marks. "There was another pallet here—someone jacked the mob's shipment—easily over a hundred million dollars' worth of crack on just one pallet.

"This must be the only guy shot in the back," McCloud called as he examined the body's bullet wound. He put a hand on him and rolled the corpse over. Nothing remarkable jumped out at first appearance. "I don't get it, Rick. He's just some street punk, same as the rest. Nothing but low-level Bratva soldiers."

McCloud looked again. "Wait. There's an X marking the spot where they dropped the body. White athletic tape on the floor with something written on it."

Diego dropped the tarp and took one step towards his partner.

"It says, 'Gotcha.'" McCloud locked eyes with Diego. "Gotcha? What do you suppose..."

The blaring ring of a cellphone interrupted them, pealing in the darkness high overhead. It triggered the explosives attached to the girdered rafters directly above the X.

McCloud looked up just in time to watch a cloud of debris and the massive bulk of the rooftop machinery smash him into a paste on the warehouse floor.

The officers all around sprang into action—adding to the chaos of the scene. Diego howled, standing riveted to his piece of the floor, locked into something that felt like slow motion.

He looked around, taking in every tiny detail of the moment; capturing it in his mind, it replayed over and over. His eyes locked on an evil, crimson orb: a bright red LED that glowed on a newly installed surveillance camera. The sleek device stood in stark contrast from the aged and rusted support pylon where it had been affixed in order to monitor that exact spot where McCloud met his demise.

Diego stared at the intense, tiny light and then at the giant, mechanical block that had killed his partner, his best friend. The thing had been spray painted bright yellow and dotted with dripping black lines to make it look like some sort of sick and twisted smiley face.

He looked back only to see the wicked light fading from dim illumination to nothingness as the camera powered off. Somewhere, someone had been watching them.

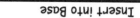

Insert into Base

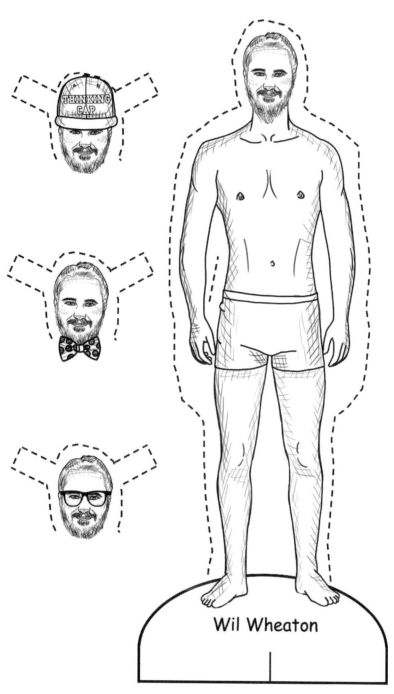

Wil Wheaton

Post pics of your weirdest scenes to
#50ShadesofWorf

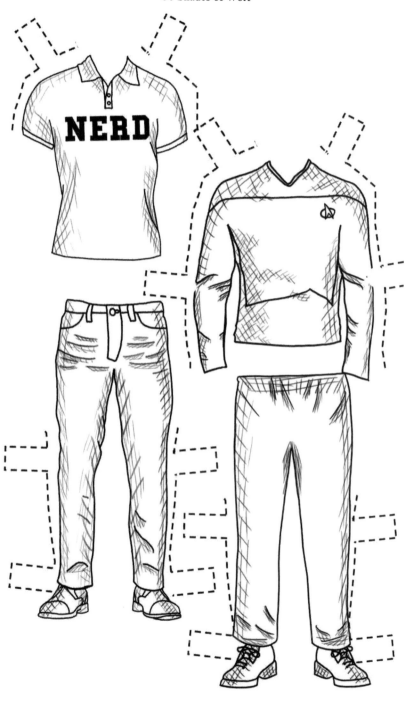

Post pics of your weirdest scenes to
#50ShadesofWorf

# PART TWO

## DOWN THE GOBLIN HOLE

# 4

## Funeral for a Friend

Dressed in black, Rick Diego stood in Captain Murphy's office. Moisture glistened on his cheekbones. They'd just come from the funeral which took place in a downpour as cliche as the undiscovered actress who'd waited his table for breakfast. The moisture wasn't from his tears. Diego's heart, like the rest of him, seemed more cut from stone than ever before. His stoic demeanor had always been his strength.

"You've got to take some time to grieve, man," Captain Murphy insisted as the casket had been lowered into the earth.

Diego only glowered at her with a face like flint. "It's been three days," he said, as if that should somehow end the conversation.

The funeral happened with such speed and privacy that it almost felt like it had never happened. Discretion was standard protocol whenever premeditation was a significant factor in an officer's death. The last thing they needed was a publicity tour given to a homicidal maniac.

His eyes narrowed. "What more do we know now after these past three days than we did within the first six hours?"

Captain Murphy's lips stretched tight.

Her door opened and a contrite officer Farnsworth walked in with two plates. The plates boasted a distinct floral pattern on the flatware. Each was piled high with snicker-doodles;

Farnsworth's face and neck flushed with private grief. He kept his eyes low and handed the plate to the confused detective.

"Sorry. I know it was closed affair, but I get bake-ey when I'm..."

Diego suspiciously eyed the plate. His gaze momentarily locked onto its floral print as he growled like an angry animal.

Farnsworth tried to squelch a slight yip and made a bee-line out the way he'd come, leaving one plate with his superiors.

The detective watched the well-wishing officer retreat to his desk. He tossed the plate on his boss's desk and it cracked in half. Only the cellophane wrapping held it together.

Murphy snapped her fingers to get his attention. "Did you even know?"

He raised an eyebrow at the question. Diego didn't know what she was talking about.

She held up a cookie and took a bite. "Snicker-doodles where McCloud's favorite."

Diego grimaced. "I didn't know he even liked cookies."

"Rick... *everyone* loves cookies." Her face softened. Diego was obviously not okay. "McCloud had a big impact on *everyone* in the precinct. We're going to find whoever was responsible. There's a whole team of us on it. You can take some time..."

He fixed his gray eyes on her and asked again, "What progress did we make in the last three days?"

Though the cookie had been delicious she tossed the remainder aside. His question turned her stomach and she refused to answer.

"That's why you need me on this case. Jared deserves justice."

Murphy's posture shifted as she assumed a superior demeanor. "Alright. Fine. You're on the case—but I'm going to assign you a partner as soon as possible. Someone to keep you in check. If I hear or even *think* you're starting to drown in the pressure of it all, you'll be off the case, understand?"

His wounded pride refused to acknowledge her concerns and he stood there, agreeing with silent defiance. "I have a few solid candidates in mind. May I make a recommendation for McCloud's replacement?"

It was Murphy's turn to wear the stone face. "No you may not. I will give you exactly who you need... not what you want."

Diego stared down his nose at her, but acknowledged the hard woman's command. This was her call and the only way he'd get to work the case. "Understood."

"Good. You've got your conditions—now go solve this murder. I'll fill you in once I have made a staffing decision."

# 5

Forensics

Diego stood at the main kiosk in the second sub-level of the police headquarters and waited for the office manager to address him. He tried to make small talk with her. "Are you guys still buried under the massive workload from the FBI?"

The mousey woman at the desk merely nodded and readjusted her glasses. "Yeah. Cyber-crimes can be pretty tedious." Her eyes scanned horizontally as she multi-tasked and tracked the lines of data on her screen; she didn't so much as look up at him. "Hafta check every little detail on this huge, local phishing scam the feds have us following up on. I hear the perps are looking at a Rico indictment."

Diego scowled. He didn't care about their work. He wasn't interested in any of the happenings in the IT dungeon—he just wanted to get someone to look into McCloud's murder. Right now, he'd settle for someone recognizing him and giving him the time of day.

He stood straighter and tried to reset his face to a neutral expression. He cleared his throat, hoping one of the basement dwellers would offer to assist him.

Across the room a short, skinny officer stood and approached. "Excuse me, are you Detective Rick Diego?"

Diego nodded.

"I'm Miles Alanon." He motioned for him to follow back to his desk. "I got your request earlier. The feds have locked us up for days on this thing, but I spent a little extra time on this, per special request from a mutual friend."

Diego followed him and noticed the officer's monitor was busy running some kind of software package that he didn't understand.

Miles tossed a bagged surveillance camera towards the detective and pushed a half-eaten plate of snicker-doodles aside as he opened his personal laptop. Moments later he'd accessed the police server and pulled up a bunch of images.

"Do you know what this is?" The screen was filled with a bunch of random letters, numbers, and other digital characters.

Diego shook his head.

"Some kind of wicked-nasty virus. Very specific and crazy deadly—technologically speaking that is." He cycled through a series of photographs taken of the unit's hardware. "Efficient, but simple. It basically revs up the hardware until everything melts down."

Turning the device over in his hands, Diego verified what he saw images of: any kind of serial numbers or identifying markers had been destroyed. More photos of a scorched computer tower followed. Engraved plates with serial numbers were similarly filed off.

"Whoever installed this camera and slaved it to the main surveillance system activated some kind of computer code that destroyed everything. There isn't any way to trace it back. Every scrap of data on the drives is shot."

"Can't you guys do some kind of computer magic and salvage any of it?" Diego stared into the dead, ruby eye of the wireless camera.

Miles shook his head. "It doesn't work like that. Most of what you see in the movies is fake... I can only tell you that whatever info we might be able to learn from any recovered data isn't likely to be useful. You'd be better off buying lottery tickets than hoping for a digital lead."

"And the phone?"

Miles pulled up a few more pictures. The mangled and charred hardware was in pieces, but some of the identifiers from the unit had survived. "A burner phone, the kind that can be purchased at any corner electronics store. The owner activated it with a phone-card bought all the way across town from it." Two keystrokes brought up the receipt bearing the card's activation numbers and the words *cash sale* at the bottom. "Sorry. It could belong to literally anyone in the city."

Diego nodded measuredly and thanked Miles for his time. He cradled the dead, cylon spy in his hands and headed back for his desk, desperate for a new lead that was more specific than *lives in the city.*

# 6

## More Than a Plateful

"You know you're not supposed to take my plates out of the house," Ethel Farnsworth berated him through the telephone.

"I know mom, it's just that we were out of paper plates…"

"Listen Moses, you know how I like to keep my plates. What if someone doesn't return one—what am I supposed to do with an incomplete set?"

"I know, I know. But I was just calling to ask if you'd gotten the mail?" He sighed and planted his forehead in his palm as she refused to change the subject, still prattling on about her plate collection.

"As long as you're still living in my house…" she continued the first movement in her concerto of condescension and finally moved into the second. "Honestly. You'd be so much better suited to any number of things. Isn't it time you gave up on being a police officer and went into something more practical?"

Moses Farnsworth rolled his eyes and spotted Detective Diego exiting the elevator. He held the surveillance equipment from the crime scene in his hand, but the grim look on his face meant it had been a dry lead.

"…Florence says so, everybody thinks it?" Ethel prattled. "You remember her—I play bridge with her and her sister on Tuesdays. Have you considered a career as an insurance salesman? Her daughter owns a small brokerage—*and she's single.*"

"Yeah. But the mail? I'm expecting my test results."

She shifted conversational gears like a trucker on the freeway.

"Nothing but a coupon for an oil change—but that reminds me that you promised to clean the gutters last weekend and now that squirrel is stuck up in there doing God knows what. I saw him with another squirrel—but aren't they like birds... males and females look different right? I hope those aren't gay squirrels. What would the neighbors say to that?"

"Yeah I've got to go," he said.

"But what about the squirrel."

"Sorry. Schwarzenegger is here with a duffel bag full of guns. I gotta go save Sarah Connor." He severed the call before she could stick another word in.

He pounded his head on his desk, knocking over an action figure. Making detective might finally give him a pay raise that would let him move out—even if that gave his mom a heart attack. Especially if that meant giving her a heart attack.

# 7

Grinning Death Machine

Captain Murphy dumped the burnt, greasy sediment from the bottom of the coffee pot into a mug and handed it to Diego who sat glumly in the staff lounge. "Just how you like it."

She hit the button to brew another pot and Diego nodded gratefully before turning his attention back to the useless security camera. His gut insisted there was some kind of clue connected to it, but he couldn't see it. A collection of crime scene photos lay spread out like a collage on the table; he'd hoped they would somehow help him decode the mystery.

Murphy tilted a plate towards him to offer him the last snicker-doodle.

He wrinkled his nose. "Never been a big fan of sugar," he muttered.

She shrugged and polished off the plate. "I bet you even have abs, too." She rolled her eyes and popped the last cookie between her lips.

The door opened and Farnsworth entered carrying a stack of paperwork. "There you guys are," the officer said. "I have the paperwork you asked for."

Murphy nodded, informally thanking and dismissing him all with one curt action. She flipped through her paperwork which included a sealed packet containing the results from the most recent detective's exams.

Farnsworth leaned sidelong to get a better angle to see the pictures of the crime scene; they'd kept the images pretty close to the vest due to the sensitive nature of the murder. "No way," Farnsworth whispered. "Quast said it was pretty crazy, and gruesome, but daaaang," he stretched his words as he goose-stepped closer to peek at the images.

Diego glared at the beat cop and ground his teeth. The officer missed all the obvious cues requesting him to leave. Diego was about to snap when Farnsworth spoke again.

"It is," the officer said to himself. "It's almost a copycat murder from the comic books."

Both Diego and Murphy stiffened and locked eyes on him.

"What do you mean?" the detective asked.

Given an unspoken invitation Farnsworth stepped up to the table. He pulled out a handful of photos and laid them out in a strange pattern. "I get why most people wouldn't see it," he rambled. "It was a pretty rare release."

Diego raised an eyebrow much like a confused vulcan.

"Oh. Right. This layout right here looks almost exactly like the alternate pages from the *Caped Defenders* finale—the variant edition of issue thirty-eight." He traced his fingers along the layout as if they retold the story.

"Here, the Grinning Man rigged a cellphone bomb to a cut girder. When the hero, Detective Grimm, arrived he found his sidekick, the Sparrow, had been murdered and left on an X to mark the spot where he'd positioned he body." He indicated a photo of the X and then tapped the camera. "The main difference is that the Grinning Man used a brightly painted grand piano with a smiley face on it... it's kind of his calling card." He quickly pulled out his mobile and showed it to the detective. The graphic had been set as his background.

"It's iconic because the Grinning Man finally killed the hero, his nemesis Detective Grimm, even if it was only in a *what-if* scenario."

Murphy tapped her lip thoughtfully as Diego stared at the krylon-yellow machinery. "You might be onto something," she said flatly.

"This comic book is rare?"

Farnsworth nodded.

"How rare?"

"Pretty limited release for the physical copies and they were only available to an exclusive club. Still it doesn't break more than a few hundred bucks because it's relatively recent, but it should become pretty valuable in the future if demand increases; supply is certainly short and it launched the whole Grinning Man series—the villain was always the star of that particular comic, anyway."

"How many folks do you suppose live in this city that have a copy of that book? Is it something that we can find out?" the Captain asked.

Shrugging, Farnsworth said, "Probably. It's rare, but there are bound to be at least a couple folks who have it."

She weighed and sifted her thoughts. "It's not like they track comic books over at the ATF or anything, but I might have a contact at the FBI who can find anyone who owns the books. Besides, they kind of owe me a favor after borrowing so many of our cyber-crime resources for their Rico case."

Farnsworth looked at her with eyebrows arched high. "They can do that?"

"You'd be surprised at what they know."

"What are they afraid of," Farnsworth nervously laughed, "some kind of nerd uprising?"

She only met his gaze with an icy, silent response. The Captain bobbed her head at Diego, "Go home and get some rest. You need to recharge and I'll have that info for you in the morning, if it exists."

He snorted gruffly, but stood.

"You'll need the extra mental energy to show him the ropes." She nodded towards the precinct's resident geek. "You're taking him with you—he's obviously onto something we didn't see. Consider him your cultural expert."

Diego shot her a betrayed look. His jaw hung slightly agape.

She flipped open her top file and indicated Farnsworth's passing grade on the detective's exam. "He's already passed the test. It's not like this assignment is permanent, but this might be exactly what you need to crack the case."

Confused, Farnsworth did a double take between the other two.

Diego squinted with ire. "You don't mean..."

Captain Murphy did everything she could not to grin as she handed the exam results to the blue-shirted officer. "Meet your new partner, *Detective* Farnsworth."

# 8

Badge #NC-1701-D

"What in the heck are you wearing?" Diego spat as Farnsworth entered the precinct.

Farnsworth ran his thumbs under the lapels of the checkered sport coat. "You said to wear a suit. It's the only one I have; it belonged to my grandpa."

Diego noted the twinkle in Officer Quast's eye as she scoped him out across the room. The senior detective put his face into the palm of his hand and mumbled a thousand curses under his breath.

"Guess I should just be glad it wasn't a Batman costume," he muttered and motioned for his new sidekick to join him in the Captain's office.

"One second," Farnsworth said as he stopped at his desk to rearrange his action figures, straightening them from their pornographic poses and returning them to their regular positions. He spotted a yellow sticky note on his monitor. Someone with an impressive amount of skill had drawn a cartoon Farnsworth in a superhero pose. *Congrats, Detective Farnsworth* it read.

He smiled, eyes searching the room for Jennifer Quast, but she had left the room. Farnsworth didn't *know* it had been her doing, but he'd hoped. He peeled the note off and put it into the notepad he kept in his lapel pocket.

Bumbling as he turned, Farnsworth tripped on the thick laces of his grandpa's dress shoes. He stumbled into his desk and banged his knee on a drawer; all of the action figures fell over as if they'd experienced an earthquake.

"Farnsworth!" Diego yelled.

He hurriedly tied the laces and left the toys to lay where they'd fallen. Finally, he joined his partner.

Captain Murphy kept a straight face when Farnsworth entered, aside from a slight eyebrow raise. She thrust the print-out into Diego's hands.

Diego scanned the document quickly and then grabbed his jacket. "Two names on the list," he said. "One is a comic book store. The other is just some random name. I'll see if I can get Quast to find an address for this Jean Luc Picard guy."

Farnsworth raised a finger. "That won't get you anywhere," he said. "He's made up."

Diego only stared at Farnsworth.

"He is—or will be—the captain of the U.S.S. Enterprise D, but not for about three more hundred years."

Responding to the blank stare from the detective, he explained. "It's from Star Trek... haven't you ever seen it on television?"

Diego shrugged. "Not my thing, I guess." He started for the door waving a binder full of notes. "We've got plenty of other leads to follow as well. Your buddy in the basement got me a list of places that sell that model of security camera. The comic shop is on the way to our first stop."

"We're going to check out *every* store? There have to be some places closer than The Goblin Hole—it's clear across town," he admitted his familiarity with the comic book shop on their list.

"Yeah, but only one of them employs an ex-con that McCloud arrested several years ago." He slapped the files into Farnsworth's hands. "Get familiar with the case," he said as the young detective bobbled the binder full of loose pages.

Farnsworth flipped open the top flap. The name Henry Sheen had been circled with a highlighter along with a prison release date that was barely three months old. He had no known relatives and only a few known contacts, most of whom were currently incarcerated.

Diego kept walking away, not looking back to check on his new partner. "We've got lots to do today," he barked as if it were an order.

# 9

Black Widow

Farnsworth looked around as the car slowed. "This isn't the way to the Goblin Hole."

Diego nodded solemnly. "I know. I've got an errand, first."

The detective's Charger pulled into a driveway in a residential section and came to a stop.

"Here. Carry this," Diego leaned towards the back seat of his car and retrieved a box. He plopped the crate onto Farnsworth's lap.

Exiting the car with his green partner in tow, Diego walked towards the front door. It opened as he approached and a dark skinned woman peered out from the entry. Her eyes were bloodshot and tinted yellow by contrast with her black skin.

"Morning, Wanda."

"Good morning, Rick," she bobbed her head and waved them inside. "Can I get you some coffee?"

"No, thank you." He walked in and nodded curtly to Farnsworth. Diego's body language seemed at ease—he was familiar with the McClouds' home. "I just came to drop off these things from Jared's desk."

Farnsworth recognized the cue and set the box onto a nearby table and noticed Wanda eyeballing him.

"Is this your new partner?"

Diego's nod bordered on a wince, as if to say "for now."

Farnsworth didn't notice. He was watching McCloud's little boy as he played with a collection of action figures on the living room carpet. Farnsworth's lips crooked into a melancholy smile.

"You know," Farnsworth turned to the widow, "your husband was one of the nicest men I've ever known. I haven't always had a lot of friends... but Detective Mc—Jared... Jared was always nice. I always kinda wanted to *be him*. I wish I could have known him better."

Wanda's eyes glistened as if she might cry had she any tears left. "Thank you for the kind words."

After a few more social niceties the detectives left the McCloud home. Farnsworth crawled into the car and clicked his seatbelt. "We could have done this anytime. I thought you were hot to get to our first lead?"

Diego glanced at him sidelong. "I wanted you to see whose shoes you were trying to step into. Do you really think you're qualified for them? Can you do this job?"

Farnsworth didn't think so. He knew his own track record as a screw up far better than anyone else, but something made him nod his head. Rather than commit to the question he said, "I passed the detectives exam." He chose not to admit that it took him three tries to do it.

Diego put the car in gear. "You better be right. Don't let them down. Don't let *me* down."

# 10

The Weiner Ejection

The clock on the dashboard read noon as the black Charger pulled to a stop in front of the listed address.

"What the heck is Comics Land?" Diego's face scrunched up as he stared across the street; he double checked the address. "Where's the Goblin Hole?"

"It's there," said Farnsworth. "It's kind of a specialty store," he explained as a seasoned pro who'd made regular visits. "They rent a separate business space in the basement of Comics Land. The Goblin Hole only deals in rare and expensive comics. It operates only by appointment and at comic book conventions. Speaking of which, did you know that there's a big convention, TrollCON, coming to…"

Diego waved him off absentmindedly as he watched the storefront across the way.

"Oh hey! A hot-dog stand. *It is* lunchtime. You want a couple dogs?" Farnsworth asked.

The senior partner looked back, pulled out of deep thought as he people-watched. "Um, yeah," he said absentmindedly, still watching the storefront. He liked to have an idea of what he might find in a place before he went in.

Both doors opened and Diego leaned against the vehicle to continue his surveillance as Farnsworth scurried down the sidewalk where the mobile food unit had set up. Diego tried not to stare. He'd walked through crack houses, gory murder scenes, and a thousand other places that would make any regular citizen cringe... but this place? A comic book store was foreign soil to him.

"I got em," Farnsworth called out as he walked back towards the car. He carried a food service boat in each hand; one had two dogs neatly prepared with the works, the other's dogs seemed as if they drowned in a sea of ketchup.

Distracted, Diego only paid Farnsworth half a mind until his clubfooted partner tripped on an uneven segment of sidewalk and hurled both boats onto Diego's chest.

Farnsworth tumbled through a roll and then jumped to his feet, cursing with apologies like an overly polite sailor. "Ohmygod! I'msosorry!"

Diego blinked slowly and managed to keep a snarl from his lips. He rolled his eyes towards the heavens as if thinking he should have expected nothing less.

The detective *did* manage to catch all of the hotdogs, even if they'd transformed his shirt into a Jackson Pollock painting. He thrust the boats back into Farnsworth's hands and exhaled his ire with one terse breath.

"Lesson number one about being a professional," Diego sighed, "always keep a spare shirt in your trunk."

Diego unbuttoned his shirt and glanced downward. Deciding it was a lost cause, he ripped it off and threw it in the street-side trash bin before popping the trunk open.

Farnsworth glanced at the man who had no fear of going topless in the middle of the city. His partner's broad torso rippled with muscles—and abs. Abs everywhere! He blushed as he nibbled awkwardly on a hot dog. Farnsworth barely had the guts to take his shirt off in the bathroom to take a shower. He took another look at his lunch and tossed half of it to a group of rowdy pigeons who strutted around a nearby bench. The fattest of the group was obviously the alpha. *Different rules for birds,* Farnsworth lamented.

Diego came back, buttoning his new shirt.

Farnsworth offered him his lunch, but Diego frowned and shook his head, no longer hungry. "Are you always this clumsy?"

"No, it was a…" he started to explain, but then hung his head. "Yes… pretty much."

Diego scowled, but did his best to turn his face away in order to keep peace with the nerd. "Well, you'd better get better, and fast. There's no place for klutzy people in the field. Maybe you should stick to the paperwork side of things and leave the physical stuff to me."

He looked back at his sheepish partner and tried to decide on the most delicate way to put it. He settled on, "Just don't get in my way," and then walked across the street with Farnsworth in hot pursuit.

# 11

The Goblin Hole

Farnsworth strolled through the aisles of comic books and pop culture merchandise with a practiced path demonstrating that he belonged there. Diego, on the other hand, scanned back and forth for danger like a whitetail deer in a        store; he tried to memorize as many faces as possible, but the overload of pasty skin and pimples quickly rendered him face-blind.

An overweight man with a stringy ponytail stood hunched over the register where he argued with the skinny man working the till. "You've got to be insane to think that Gal Gadot's Wonder Woman is anywhere near as hot as Jessica Nigri's! Hey—you don't think Nigri will be at the con next week, do you?"

"In your wettest dreams, maybe," the clerk spat.

The chunky guy cleared his throat as Farnsworth approached. "Hey... speaking of Jessicas. Where have you been, Moses? Jessica's been asking about you lately... something about you two and a..."

"Not now, James." Farnsworth cut him off and nodded backwards to Diego. "My partner and I are here on some police business. Do you have a few minutes, Newt?"

"Partner?" James scoffed. "Congratulations. You finally came out of the closet!"

"Maybe he just forgot his uniform?"

Diego completed his approach and towered over the chunky James like a T-800.

James turned to look up and into Diego's face. The big guy scowled menacingly. James gulped and then stepped aside.

Diego pulled his badge from his pocket. "Detective Rick Diego, homicide."

Newt stuttered, "H-homicide?"

Farnsworth nodded. "Really, I just need to ask if anyone's down in the Goblin Hole."

"Not today. Casey's got me watching over it like most days. He's pretty busy, you know, with the whole movie project." His voice brimmed with excitement. "Are you in on the Kickfunder campaign for *Knights of the Illuvian Age*?"

Farnsworth nodded and his eyes twinkled. "Of course! Did you see who they've secured for the role of Jarek the Ranger?"

"Did I? He's going to be here for a promo piece before the con!"

Diego leaned forward. "A-hem. We need to see the sales records, mister..."

"Jim Newton. Everybody who knows me calls me Newt." He turned to James, "Watch the counter for me, would ya?"

The sluggard nodded and stepped behind the counter to fill in. As the regular counter jockey weaved through the displays and headed towards the back while explaining how he owned Comics Land but let a friend operate out of his extra space.

Newt led the detectives through a door that led to the basement. He flipped the lights on and they descended into the dungeon. Mostly, it was just a large room populated with racks of additional shelving, bagged and cased comics displaying prices and graded ratings, and newly produced marketing materials for the *Knights of the Illuvian Age* film. The freshly cut posters and cardboard displays gave off a new-book smell that battled against the musty odor of the poorly ventilated basement.

"Here we are," Newt said, stepping behind a glass case with a vinyl banner that read *The Goblin Hole*. "Now what's this about a murder?" he asked nervously.

Before Farnsworth could speak, Diego plainly stated, "We just need to know if anyone has purchased a comic book that might be related to the incident." He looked at Farnsworth with eyes that indicated he should be cautious with details.

"Do you still have the *Caped Defenders* number thirty-eight variant edition?" Farnsworth asked.

"Lemme check," Newt said, turning a circle and scanning the racks. "Yup. There it is." He pointed to the sealed, plastic display case. The cover graphic was almost entirely filled with the yellow piano, except for the red splatters at the bottom, and painted with the Grinning Man's smiley face.

"Looks like Casey is only asking six hundred bucks for it," Newt said. "Pretty good deal, but I bet he'd knock off twenty bucks if you wanted to take it home today. You want me to call him?"

"No." Diego said, turning to leave. He didn't have time for dead ends. "But give us the owner's contact info in case I have further questions."

Newt shrugged and jotted down the contact info for Casey Kubrick.

The detective scanned it as he glanced at the *Knights of the Illuvian Age* materials. It listed Casey Kubrick as the director.

Newt caught his eyes. "He's a relative of the great one: Stanley Kubrick. Says he learned all about the movies from him."

Diego's face remained unchanged. He pocketed the contact information. "Thanks for your time."

Farnsworth followed his partner out of the store.

Diego breathed a sigh of relief as he cleared the sidewalk, finally able to breathe again, as if he'd just spent twenty minutes in Oz walking a yellow brick road that went nowhere. "Who is Jessica?"

Farnsworth stiffened. "Nigri? The famous cosplayer?"

"Cos-what? No... the other one. The one the fat guy with the mullet mentioned."

"Oh. Uh... she's no one." Farnsworth blushed slightly.

"Sure," Diego said sarcastically and they got in the car.

# 12

A Lead

The door of the corner electronics store chimed as it opened and the two detectives walked in. Two employees looked up from behind the counter. The younger of the two mens' faces fell and he stepped onto the sales floor of the small chain store.

"I got these guys, Stanley."

Stanley nodded and went back to mindlessly tapping and swiping on his smart-phone which he held ridiculously close to his face. It chirped with Candy Crush chimes.

Diego and the younger man kept eyes locked, and then the detective veered hard right and started rummaging through the stock of prepaid mobile phones. He held one out and then spun a small carousel holding the stock of re-loadable phone service cards that the burner phones needed to access a network.

"Do you sell a lot of these, Henry?"

"Mobile phones? Um, yeah. Not a lot of people in this part of town who have good enough credit for regular service plans."

Diego narrowed his eyes. "I mean *this exact model*."

Farnsworth watched as Henry shrugged. He observed every detail of the exchange while he meandered through the nearby aisles.

"Where were you five mornings ago?"

Henry's eyes opened wide with anxiety. "I was right here." He looked over his shoulder at Stanley. "Just don't ask *him*. Stanley's my boss; he don't know that I got a record."

"Or that you have a parole officer?" Diego's voice was several decibels louder than previous, threatening to spill the worker's secret if he didn't cooperate.

Henry shushed him and glanced back to make sure that Stanley hadn't bothered to pay close attention. *"What do you want?"* he hissed. "I can't lose this job!"

"You know anything about Detective McCloud's murder?"

Henry shook his head.

"But you knew he was killed."

"Word travels quick on the street—especially bout people who earned lots of enemies." Henry glanced nervously at Farnsworth who slowly stalked the merchandise aisle parallel to the phones. "Who's he?"

"Someone with inside information on the case. Someone who was very close to McCloud and knows all sorts of details. This guy... he's a real psycho," Diego feigned nervousness. "Even *I'm* terrified of this guy and what he might do."

Farnsworth squinted and jutted out his jaw slightly so that the edges of his incisors showed. He played the part, silently glad for all the role playing games he'd participated in during his youth... and adult years.

Henry turned his gaze back to Diego. "I don't know anything, man. I'm shooting straight with you."

Stanley wandered away from the register. "Is there something I can help you gentlemen find?"

Diego flashed his badge. "These security cameras," he said. "Do you sell a lot of them? This specific model was found at a nearby murder scene. We were just asking mister Sheen here about them."

The older manager nodded, eager to share his useless knowledge of the gadgetry. "Well, they're a pretty new model. They just came out about two months ago... nice little unit, but a bit too pricey for this market." He bobbed his head to the stack of the boxes on the end-cap. "We only stock them because the franchise makes us keep so many on hand."

Farnsworth walked towards the boxes as his partner asked the questions.

"How many of these have you sold? Do you have records for anyone who's bought them?"

Stanley chuckled. "Oh, we haven't sold a single one. We'll probably end up sending them back to corporate as soon as possible, just like I told that upper management mucky muck I'd do. Waste of time in a store like mine."

"See, detective. You won't find any leads here. It's like I said…"

Farnsworth tripped on a shoelace and crashed through the stack of camera boxes, sending them scattering across the floor. He grunted a string of apologies as he scrambled to his hands and feet.

Diego sighed and rolled his eyes at his partner's toddler-like performance. Stanley recoiled, mortified by the scene.

The klutzy detective picked up a box that he'd crushed; it had been at the bottom of the merchandise display. Farnsworth held it up and dangled it in front of the others. He shook the flattened container and only packing supplies fell out. "This box was empty," Farnsworth said, nearly out of breath.

Diego snapped his attention back to Henry.

Henry's eyes lit up like lightning and everyone knew that he'd been aware of it. The ex-con dumped a shelf between him and the detective and bolted for the back door.

Chasing him towards the rear, Diego leapt over the collapsed shelving. Farnsworth tried to join the pursuit; he ran as graceful as a newborn calf. The detectives converged on the door nearest the rear exit and ducked inside the stockroom.

Farnsworth bumped into a shelf of used computer monitors. The tower of electronics tumbled onto his partner and sent him sprawling under an avalanche of old screens that should have been disposed of decades ago.

He grunted and crawled out from the wreckage. Diego finally joined Farnsworth in the alley. His confused partner looked back and forth with indecision, unsure which way to go.

Diego's anger simmered near the top, but he held his tongue and snorted with displeasure.

Their lead suspect had escaped—but at least they had a solid lead.

# 13

Steak Dinner

Rick Diego's Charger pulled onto the block where Henry Sheen's apartment was located. They'd already called in a warrant and spotted a few squad cars pulling up to secure the area ahead of the eight-plex's manager.

The swarthy man jangled a thick set of keys and waddled down the sidewalk like a human bulldozer in a twice-pawned gold chain. Jennifer Quast followed him a step behind, moving in her awkward way with arms that barely moved; despite the mousey demeanor, her eyes sparkled when they locked on the Charger.

Diego shook his head and almost chuckled. He imagined that Farnsworth's chances with the ladies would shoot through the roof with his promotion... maybe also by sitting in a car like this.

"Do you see it?" Farnsworth asked.

"What do you mean?" Diego saw that Quast noticed something too and followed her eyes. The bumper and grill of a white box truck peeked out from a partially collapsed structure a block down the way.

"It matches the description of the missing Union Industries vehicle... at least, it looks like it from here."

Diego pulled the car to a stop. "Go check it out."

"Where are you going?" Farnsworth asked with a slight waver in his voice.

"To shake down an informant who might have something for me. Get one of the officers, or maybe Quast, to give you a ride back."

"Wait. What am I supposed to do in the apartment?"

Diego looked at his partner. "You're a detective, now. Detect something." He booted him out the door and sped down the street. Quast watched the car go.

Finally, she and Farnsworth turned and strolled down the block while the uniformed officers secured the apartment; Sheen probably wasn't stupid enough to return home after fleeing this morning.

"Exciting first day?" Quast tried to make small talk.

"Yup."

The awkwardness was palpable.

"Diego's shirt is different." Her voice remained as monotone as ever, just another endearing trait.

He always found her attention to small details remarkable. "Yup... there was a hot dog incident."

"Of course there was."

They walked the rest of the way in silence.

Coming upon the truck they peeked into the crumbling structure. A bunch of rotted beams had fallen onto the cargo hauler that had been crammed into too small of a space.

Farnsworth crouched under a few sheafs of fallen boards. He had to suck in his gut to squeeze through, but got a view of the faded graphic wrap. "Union Industries. It's our missing truck alright."

Quast recorded it in her notebook and then they walked back towards the apartment.

"I'm glad you got the job. McCloud's job," she clarified. "I spend a lot of time in the file room."

Farnsworth knew that. Everyone knew that—it was her attention to detail and ability to find things others missed that had earned her the post as an analyst.

"We're all cops, but not everyone is nice." She kept her gaze on the sidewalk and her shoulders perfectly straight so that her arms wouldn't swing.

Quast continued speaking in her meek, almost squeaky voice. "Once, a bunch of officers wrote my name on a dog dish and left it in the file room. I know..." her voice wavered, "I know I'm not like all the other girls. Quirky people... we know we're weird. But that was just plain mean."

"You're not weird," Farnsworth insisted.

Quast ignored him. "Detective McCloud found out who it was and yelled at them. Not like how angry people yell—but like how scary people do it: quietly... with terrifying calm. I got an apology card with a gift certificate for a steak dinner after that." She momentarily stopped walking and curled her lips into something like a wounded smile. "I recognized his writing. I know McCloud wrote the card... He always made things better."

Finally, Jenny Quast looked up and at Farnsworth. "McCloud was nice. I hope you stay more like him. Don't try to be like Diego. Rick Diego is fine and all, but he is... you should just stay like *you*." She looked back down and hurried up the steps to the suspect's apartment.

Farnsworth nodded and touched the pocket where he kept the sticky note she'd drawn for him and then followed her up the stairs. He halted right behind her and stood at the door where the grumpy-looking landlord paced nervously.

The apartment had been tossed; Sheen's mail and anything of value lay strewn across the floor, including a single ticket to TrollCON. Furniture lay cut open and anything with an ounce of fragility lay busted on the faux-woodgrain linoleum.

On the door which hung ajar, a butterfly knife lodged deep into the wood. It pierced a photograph of Henry Sheen, pinning it to the door at eye level.

He and Quast both frowned at the sign. It was Gage Houdek's calling card, and once the notorious mob hit-man had marked a target, he had never failed to score the kill.

# 14

Davey

A couple of clean-cut frat boys walked down the hallway of the sprawling housing complex. They turned their faces away from Detective Diego who had clipped his badge to his belt so there was no mistaking him.

"Aren't you guys going to be late for class?" He grinned as they hurried past him as quickly as possible without incriminating themselves.

Diego rapped on the apartment door they'd just come from. It opened and caught on the end of the security chain revealing a man in his mid-twenties.

The man behind the door sighed when he recognized Diego.

"Hello Davey."

"What do *you* want?" Davey moaned.

"I just want to chat for a few minutes. Should I wait out here all day and scare away your customers until you've got some free time… or is now good?"

"Hold up." Davey closed the door.

Several long moments passed before the drug dealer slid the chain back and opened up. Diego assumed he spent them hiding anything that could incriminate and by texting his clients to delay any pickups by an hour or so.

Davey swung the door wide open. "Well, don't keep me waiting."

Diego stepped inside and spotted a woman in a wheelchair. She sat slouched and staring at the television, borderline nonresponsive. "Glad to see your sister's still doing okay." He quickly cased the joint. "Aside from your extra-curricular activities you seem to be holding up just fine."

Davey scowled in response; he held the power button on his phone, forcing it to shut all the way down in case the police demanded access. He knew his rights. "What do you want?" He furrowed his brow like an animal corralled in its den. "You should know better than to come here."

Diego's voice came like a menacing growl. "Someone killed my partner a few days ago and I'm going to find out who it was. I need info to do that. What do you know about the big cocaine shipment that fell apart a few days ago?"

Davey shrugged placidly. "You know I don't deal with those kinds of drugs. I only play with the fun stuff those rich college kids like: that hoity-toity crowd I used to run with before I lost my scholarships."

"Yeah. *I know* that. But I know that you keep your ear to the street. Someone killed my partner. How would you react if someone hurt *her?*" He bobbed his head to Davey's crippled sister.

"Not so good," he mumbled.

"Exactly. Now find out what I need to know."

"What if I can't get no info?"

Diego scowled. "You'd better try, cuz if I don't find out what the street knows, it's gonna get rough for you and every other CI that I press. I'm not gonna tell your PO; I'll just let it slip that you've been my snitch for the last three years and let the street take care of itself."

"You wouldn't do that, would you?" Nervousness worked its way into his voice like a corkscrew. "Who else you gonna turn to when you need information? You wouldn't really burn me like that?"

The stone-faced detective only glowered. "You'd be surprised of what I'm capable of when someone hurts my friends."

Ashen faced, Davey swallowed the hard lump in his throat and nodded slowly. "I'll see what I can find out."

"You do that. Call me when you have something."

Davey stuck his hand out as if to shake. "We—we're friends, right?"

Diego left him hanging and turned to leave. "That's going to depend on the next few days." The detective let the door shut behind him and he heard his informant reattach the security chain.

# 15

Motivation

Diego raised his stack of paperwork and dropped it onto Farnsworth's desk. The impact rocked the posed action figures back and forth; the Incredible Hulk tipped over and fell into the wastebasket.

The feat made Diego smile, but he did retrieve the toy and put it back in place.

Farnsworth opened up the stack and began scanning the papers with his eyes. He made a few minor corrections with his ink pen. Diego raised an eyebrow at the necessary alterations to the documents. Farnsworth handed his partner a short stack of his own.

"What we found in Sheen's apartment."

Diego flipped through it. Aside from a few empty baggies that confirmed Sheen had been either selling or using crack—probably selling—there was little else to implicate him... except that the truck stolen from the crime scene was nearby. "Any evidence tying Sheen to the truck?" he asked. It was an obvious tie, but there was no direct proof. Yet.

"They found some hair samples in the cab. Quast sent them to the lab for testing. We should know by tomorrow."

"Quast, huh?"

Farnsworth shot him an apprehensive look. "Of course—she's the best at this kind of stuff."

"You think Quast is the best?" He let his tough veneer crack for a moment and even flashed him a roguish smile.

"Yes... I mean... she's a fine analyst—I mean excellent officer," he spat, flustered.

"Relax, Farnsworth. I'm just giving you crap." He took a seat at the desk and turned to the photo of the butterfly knife. "It does seem like we're not the only ones looking for Sheen."

Farnsworth pulled up a file on his computer. It showed a number of similar knives through photos. All of the subsequent photos of victims had been attributed to Gage Houdek. Zmei. "It does seem to indicate we're up against a pro."

Diego nodded slowly, intentionally. "Listen," he tried to force as much compassion into his voice as possible. "With a professional assassin at large, it might not be for the best if you accompany me into the field. I'd prefer not having to watch out for..." he trailed off and pointed at the on-screen murder weapons, trying to make it about safety.

Farnsworth didn't respond.

"You know... it's just that, well, you're kind of..."

"A screw up? Clumsy? Yeah, I know. But that was also what led to us outing Sheen." He fixed Diego with an intense stare that the larger man had never seen. "I promise you, nothing scares me more than letting you down."

Diego's lips tightened and he blinked slow. "Okay." He sighed, "Make sure that you don't." His pocket vibrated and the detective withdrew his phone to check the text.

It came from Davey.

"People work quick when properly motivated," he mumbled, silently wondering exactly how he could motivate his partner to become everything McCloud had ever been.

He read the address and pushed the paperwork across the desk. "Log this. I've got to go meet one of my CIs. I'll fill you in when I get back."

Farnsworth didn't have time to protest the scut work. Before he could open his mouth, Diego was already gone.

# 16

Enter Wil Wheaton

Moses Farnsworth looked up from his desk and his jaw fell open. Walking through the precinct and trailing Captain Murphy followed an otherwise normal man; his graphic tee peeked out from beneath his black sport coat. Farnsworth recognized the shirt as a Kickfunder swag item for the *Knights of the Illuvian Age* campaign. But he hadn't received his yet.

Farnsworth gulped hard. This was no mere commoner, he was Wil Wheaton: a giant among men! Figuratively speaking, anyways, Farnsworth knew his wikipedia entry listed him as five eleven, two inches taller than the detective.

He crept to his feet to get a glimpse of the icon who the detective knew was in town as a part of the huge, upcoming comic convention. Farnsworth smiled at him from his workstation, but Wheaton's eyes scanned right past him, not stopping to linger on the colorful array of plastic figures arranged at the desk.

Between that and the tight-lipped expression on his face, Farnsworth guessed that Wheaton had something serious on his mind. The celebrity slipped his jacket off and tossed it on the back of a chair in the Captain's office.

As graceful and silent as a cat with wooden legs, Farnsworth rushed to the door to eavesdrop. He didn't catch a whole lot, but he heard enough. Someone had defaced his hotel door—

they'd stabbed a photo of the actor onto it using a butterfly knife.

Farnsworth's gut plunged into his stomach at the implication. *Houdek is gonna kill Wil Wheaton!*

The inelegant detective jumped behind a fake shrubbery that hid nearly fifteen percent of his body when he heard movement towards the door.

Murphy escorted Wheaton out. Neither realized that he'd left his sport coat behind.

She glanced Farnsworth's direction but said nothing about the pudgy officer failing a stealth check behind the plastic ficus. "So sorry about this; but you can rest assured that the Chief of Police has a personal interest in this case and he has put me in charge of securing your safety. We'll get your room changed and set up anonymously in a new hotel. We'll also put a couple of uniformed officers standing guard."

The Captain returned a few minutes later to find Farnsworth hovering near her door. His suit coat had magically transformed colors. It did not fit well.

She eyed him up and down. "What's got you so antsy? I haven't seen someone do this same little dance thing you're doing since my nephew had to wait to use a restroom."

"Permission to be assigned to watch Wil Wheaton's hotel room?"

Murphy gave him a skeptical look. "Farnsworth, you're not a uniformed officer anymore. You're a detective. Now go take a leak and get back to work." She moved on but turned to warn him. "Make sure that you don't tell anyone about Zmei—especially not whoever this Wheaton guy is—I don't remember nobody 'cept Spock and Captain Kirk from Star Wars…"

"Star Trek."

"Whatever. But make sure he doesn't suddenly think there's a hit-man chasing him."

"Isn't there a hit-man chasing him?"

*"We don't know that.* It could be a coincidence or a copycat. Why would the Bratva want to kill a washed up child actor anyway? It doesn't make any sense."

"Washed up? *Big Bang Theory, Geek and Sundry, Gorgeous Tiny Chicken Machine Show*? He's been in all kinds of TV shows."

She shot him a worried look. "I'm beginning to think you've got way too much free time on your hands, Farnsworth."

He wilted beneath her gaze.

"Not a peep until there's something concrete to link Wheaton to the Russian mob situation."

Bobbing his head like a punished child, Farnsworth returned to his desk. When nobody was looking, he pulled the breast lapel of his new jacket to his nose and took a deep sniff.

# 17

The Snitch

Davey walked out of the convenience store and nodded towards the sleek, black Charger. He glanced around quickly to make sure nobody around him might recognize the vehicle.

The locks popped and he slid into the passenger seat.

"What have you got for me, Davey?"

Diego kept his eyes on the road as he navigated the streets.

"Pssh," Davey hissed. "Treat me like you do, and you roll up in here like you're doing me a favor." He crossed his arms as if he wouldn't give up the information. Both men knew that it was a front for his wounded pride.

"Nah," Diego grinned. "You're gonna tell me everything I want, and more."

Davey chuckled and shook his head. "Pretty sure of yourself for some reason."

Diego looked over at him. "Of course you want to help me. Cuz we're friends, now."

"Friends? What you ever do for me?" He was about to build a house on shore of false bravado when Diego handed him a business card.

Davey turned it over in his hands, an appointment card with a date and time listed for Monday. "HM Medical Supply. What is this—some kinda joke? Maybe another threat?"

"Your sister," he kept his eyes on the road, "she's been stuck on the waiting list for a long time, right? Been eight months now... they just keep pushing her down the list even though they're supposed to take state medical, right?"

He took Davey's silence as a confirmation.

"I called in a favor. Talked to a few friends. You bring her to that appointment; they're going to make it right and get her taken care of."

Davey turned his head to look out the window, angling his face away from Diego's so the cop couldn't see his eyes moisten.

"You know that I can be persuasive. *I'm* not the bad guy here. *You're* not the bad guy, Davey. The clinic's not the bad guy—your *sister* is *certainly* not the bad guy. That guy is the one who killed my partner: all signs point to Henry Sheen."

Davey broke the silence a minute later, once he felt sure that his voice wouldn't crack. "I know all about it—what's going down with Sheen. You're not going to like it."

"I already don't like it," Diego grouched.

The informant nodded. "The Bratva Brotherhood is involved. Sheen's old cellmate has been talking. He hooked back up with em to do some small-time stuff when he got out. Driving a truck here and there."

"The Russian mob connection explains why Houdek is back in town, but we already figured that."

Davey shot his driver a fearful look. "Zmei's involved? You make sure you keep my name out of *everything*... if 'The Dragon's' involved, I don't want nothing to do with this."

Diego shook his head and Davey rubbed the stress from his face.

Sighing, he continued. "Guess I shoulda guessed as much. Bratva just lost almost a *billion* dollars. Dunno if you realized it, but that was a lot of crack... was supposed to get shopped all across the states from here."

Diego smiled and tightened his grip on the wheel.

"Here's what I heard. Someone, Sheen, hit a weak link in the distribution network. Stole an entire pallet of cocaine and left the rest for you guys to impound... it was supposed to get shipped off to a bunch of other cities for distribution. As much as *you got*, Sheen or whoever it was got away with *a metric ton* of cocaine.

"Crazy thing is, they not only lost all of that product, but the mob can't even resupply."

"What do you mean?"

"Sheen sold it. Rock-bottom, clearance sale prices. Moved the entire shipment between his prison contacts and other locals. Straight up fifty cents on the dollar and now the candymen own their own product. Musta been planning this for a while."

Diego scrunched his face. He hadn't taken Sheen for so smart of a criminal.

"That sort of arrangement totally cuts out the Bratva. With the market flooded they won't have ground here again for months until the market saturation dries up." Davey spoke with the savvy entrepreneurial bent that college promoters had originally taken him for.

The detective understood the play. "And how did they afford to buy it from Sheen? The pushers all stole that initial investment from the Bratva to pay Sheen, hoping that in all the chaos they would never be caught at the street level."

"Exactly!" Davey laughed and slapped the dash with his palm. "Not only are they out the cash from their huge shipment, but they also took a hit when the street nickle and dimed them to buy new, stolen product off of Sheen."

Diego did the mental math and raised his eyebrows. "That's a lot of nickels."

"A hundred mil," Davey nodded.

"No wonder they're sending in Houdek to clean house." He glanced at his phone and read the text from his partner.

*Houdek marked a comic con celeb. No apparent connection... yet.* Diego responded, *Be back soon.*

Davey nodded and pointed at a corner to indicate his stop. "Zmei," he whispered almost inaudibly as if speaking the Dragon's name might summon him. He shuddered. "Do me a favor, friend?"

Diego pulled over and looked at Davey.

"Don't contact me again until this thing blows over."

# 18

The Hot-dog Revisitation

Diego strolled back into the precinct and found Farnsworth feverishly working on some research. He paused in front of the desk and tilted his head, wondering about the new, ill-fitting suit coat.

Farnsworth had covered his yellow legal pad with dates and numbers as he stared at the computer screen.

Trying to decipher the man's chicken scratchings, Diego leaned over further and caught a glimpse of the monitor. *Comic books.* Circled at the top of the page he'd written *T.G.H. sales. All @ CGC 9.9+.*

*All American #16. $45,000*
*Action #7. $101,000*
*Detective #33. $40,000*
*Pep #22. $65,000*
*TMNT 1/84. $4,000*
*Spidey 252. $2,000*
*TWD 1. $6,000*
*Amazing Fantasy 15. $300,000*
*Showcase #22. $22*
*Inc. Hulk #181. $55,000*

The list continued. Diego cleared his throat and startled Farnsworth. He looked up.

"Oh. Uh... just doing a little research."

Diego shrugged. He didn't understand the list but didn't think it was pressing, considering what he'd learned from Davey. He began explaining what he'd heard from his informant when Farnsworth opened a drawer and retrieved a foam take-out container.

He set it gingerly on the desk and slid it towards his partner as if it might explode.

Diego opened it and found two hot dogs.

"I figured I still owed you these."

With a constipated expression that bordered on a smile, Diego bobbed his head appreciatively. His stomach growled in thanks; he hadn't eaten anything all day.

Diego finished bringing Farnsworth up to speed on the solid Bratva-Sheen connection as he crammed the food into his mouth.

Farnsworth followed along. He handed his partner a cola and explained the situation from the hotel as he heard it from Captain Murphy.

"We've got to save Wil Wheaton," Farnsworth insisted.

"They put some uniforms at the hotel. That should scare Houdek off for now."

"Yeah." Farnsworth furrowed his brow, secretly hoping the officers were better at their jobs than he had been. Knocking over stacks of used electronics and spilling lunches wouldn't be effective at keeping The Dragon and the Bratva at bay. "I hope so."

"It's probably just a coincidence, anyway." He stood and glanced at the clock. "We've got a long day tomorrow. Hopefully Davey gave us enough to go on—we'll see what the Mob has been sniffing at; that might help us narrow down where Sheen is hiding." He drained his soda and tossed the can into the wastebasket.

Farnsworth bobbed his head and pulled out an energy drink and bag of Cheetos from his drawer. "Yeah. I'll take off soon." He turned his face back to the screen. "I'm just going to look into a hunch I had for a little bit longer before I head out. It's probably nothing, but I want to check into it further."

Diego eyed him suspiciously, but shrugged and left him to it.

A few minutes after his partner left, Farnsworth shoveled his notes and all of the snacks into an environmentally conscious burlap shopping bag and hurried towards the elevator.

Farnsworth exited through the high-tech cloister in the bowels of the building and started putting the snacks on an available desk. Miles joined him moments later and sat in the office chair. He took a full spin and grinned, cracking his knuckles.

"You know this is illegal, right?" the computer specialist asked.

"You don't think we'll get caught, do you?" Farnsworth asked nervously. "What will they do to…"

"Oh please. I'm just telling you to live a little. There's no way I'm going to get caught," Miles said cockily. "There's a reason those feds came to *this station* to get help… I'm the best there is at what I do—and what it do isn't very nice." He cracked his knuckles as he growled the last bit. "Now tell me about this hunch of yours and point me at my targets."

A custom protocol window hovered open on Miles' screen. It was just a few clicks away from beginning its commands and forcing its way through digital security walls.

Farnsworth took out a list of online handles and slid them to Miles. "I want to know all about each one of these people." He cracked open his energy drink. "It's gonna be a long night."

Miles shook his head with amused disagreement. "This is probably going to be a whole lot easier than you think."

# 19

The Hangover

"Where the heck is Farnsworth?" Diego asked. He punctuated the question with a hot cup of coffee that sloshed over the edge, but just barely. "It's too early for this nonsense," he groused, searching the man's desk.

The detective sat at Farnsworth's desk, looking for a clue. His chair wasn't warm, and Farnsworth's notepad was nowhere in sight.

He glanced at the wastebasket. A cola can remained on top; it hadn't been taken out. Diego raised an eyebrow and opened Farnsworth's desk drawer. Neither wastebasket nor drawer had a bag of Cheetos or the flashy can of his partner's energy drink.

Diego guessed his partner couldn't have stuck around long after he'd left. He glanced at the clock. Farnsworth was definitely late.

Spotting Quast's ungainly approach Diego stuck his neck out. "Hey? You seen Farnsworth? He didn't, you know, maybe take you out last night or something?"

She clammed up, blushing and trying to hide a smirk. "Noooo." Quast didn't let go of his attention. "I actually came to find *you*. We got a hit on someone matching Sheen's description." She handed him an address on a paper slip. "Walking west, on foot."

Diego looked at the ceiling as he pondered a mental map. "Maybe Farnsworth was onto something. Sheen's heading from the scummy side of town towards the commercial area... Comics Land," he finally landed on a probably location. "He had one of those TrollCON tickets when you turned his apartment, right?"

Quast nodded.

As he tried to leave, she grabbed his arm. "There's more. Another homicide just called in this morning." She put the report into his hands. "Nothing special about him except that he was killed with a certain butterfly knife that was left at the scene. I've got officers on their way to check it out."

He looked at them, but with only half interest; he barely caught Quast's doodle of a butterfly with knives for feet. Diego thrust them back at Quast. Everything in Diego's gut urged him towards the door so he could chase Sheen. "Can you be my eyes and ears on those scenes? Text me the details and we'll catch up this afternoon. I've gotta catch Sheen."

He twirled his keyring on his fingers and left her hanging mid-sentence. Hurrying to his car, his phone rang: Farnsworth.

"Where the heck are you?"

"Sorry. Crazy night—I didn't get a wink of sleep,"

"What, did you get caught up reading comics under the bed covers with your flashlight?" He slammed the car door shut.

Farnsworth launched into a rapid-fire synopsis of his night. "I got so much done—I figured out why Houdek wants to kill Wil Wheaton—at least I think so. And then I went out to celebrate with the boys. I musta had a whole beer and got totally wasted! I guess the bar was some kind of S&M place or something and it was Brony night, but some dude showed up wearing cat ears and it almost turned into a riot and then the..."

"Yeah I get it!" his engine roared to life. "Save Wil Wheaton or whatever. In the meantime we got a hit on Sheen. I think he's heading towards that comic book store."

"That all makes sense," Farnsworth said.

Diego didn't pay much attention. Whatever his partner was onto wouldn't matter unless they actually caught the guy, first. He weaved his car through traffic at unsafe speeds. "Where are you? I'll be at the shop in less than ten."

"On the bus. I'm close. Less than five minutes."

"Good," Diego barked as he swerved. "You keep a lookout. Just observe; if you see him do not engage."

"Copy that, Red Leader."

Diego shook his head and tossed the phone onto the passenger seat, sure he'd missed some kind of reference. He just hoped Farnsworth had the sense to do as he was told.

The detective stepped on the gas. He had a score to settle with Henry Sheen and he didn't want to miss the settling up.

# 20

Eye of Newt

The black Charger rolled to a stop across the street from Comics Land and parked in a No Parking Zone. No other spots remained open. As Farnsworth slipped into the cab Diego saw why. The place was a madhouse; people were clamoring to get in. A sign posted in the huge front windows read "Meet Wil Wheaton, star of the upcoming film *Knights of the Illuvian Age.*" The date listed today.

"You upgrade your clothes?" Diego asked.

Farnsworth only smiled. He still wore the black sport coat but had swapped out his footwear for a garish pair of red Chuck Taylors which he'd double knotted. Tossing his small duffel into the backseat, he pointed across the street.

"Newt's at the door? He ought to be behind the till."

"What's in the bag?" Diego asked his partner, spotting the scrawny comic book store manager. He appeared almost frantic, searching the street for someone. The Detective watched the streets, not sure what he was looking for, but he suspected Newt might be waiting for Henry Sheen.

Farnsworth glanced at the bag. "A spare shirt," he said, as if it should've been obvious. He slapped down a paper print out on the dash.

"What's that?" Diego barely glanced at it, not wanting to take his eyes off of Newt and the store.

"Don't you check your email in the mornings? It's the DNA sample on the hairs found in the truck. They belong to Sheen."

Diego cursed beneath his breath and began scanning the sidewalk with renewed interest "I'm gonna mess him up for this. It proves he killed Jared."

"Well, not quite," Farnsworth said. "It just proves he was in the truck at some point—most likely the getaway when somebody whacked the Bratva pushers."

Motioning for him to continue his thoughts, he finally glanced back when Farnsworth didn't have anything else to share. "He's still our most likely suspect."

Farnsworth nodded. That much was true.

"I was up late, celebrating..."

"Yeah. Boneys and cat people or whatever. I really don't want to know that much about your weird personal life..." Diego had turned back to the busy sidewalk.

"No," Farnsworth hissed, *"before all that.* I think I found a comic con connection. You told me how much cash they'd turned the drugs into—but what can a guy do with all of that money?"

"Spend it."

"No! You can't just spend it, and besides, you've got to get out of town and fast. They brought in *Gage friggin Houdek!* You'd never stay alive long enough to spend it. You've got to launder the cash and flee the country. They're obviously planning to do that, that's why they sold the product off so quickly and in the way that they did."

Diego furrowed his brows. "You think you know how they're doing it?"

"I do. And it's why they're after him." He pointed to the poster sized mockup of Wil Wheaton standing in the window. The cardboard cut-out held an immense sword that defied Wheaton's logical wrist strength.

The larger man followed Farnsworth's finger. Cutting a path directly across where Farnsworth had pointed, strolled Henry Sheen.

Sheen kept looking behind himself as if he felt someone was following him. He kept his hands in his pockets and had a ball-cap pulled down tightly, but there was no mistaking him.

"Let's go get this guy!" Farnsworth said excitedly.

Diego held up a hand. "Not quite yet. Let's see who Newt is waiting for."

The criminal closed in on Newt and they traded a glance that indicated they were familiar, but Sheen slipped past him.

"Oh, Newt's obviously waiting for James Lee Anderson."

"Why does that name seem familiar? Did he kill a president or something?"

"You met him once before. Obnoxious guy with the nasty pony tail. Shady, creepy vibes... he steals chicken nuggets if you're not watching and cheats at Magic the Gathering. That pretty much tells you everything you need to know about him. But he also helps Newt work the door whenever there's a line for a big event, which is only a few times per year."

Newt scowled and finally went inside. Farnsworth continued. "Once, Newt thought they'd booked Stan Lee for a big event. Huge line. James Lee tried to charge an extra admission and just about got beat up by a soccer mom when it turned out to be just some regular dude named Stan Lee who produced really bad indie comics and... Oh. We're going now."

Farnsworth slipped out of the door and followed his partner across the street. He mumbled to himself, "And it's pronounced Bro-neez, thank you very much."

# 21

Contact

Farnsworth had little trouble spotting his partner in the crowd of unwashed nerds. Diego stood a full head taller than most of the eager fans packing out the comic shop.

A skinny guy stood on a small platform that had been hastily constructed for him and the celebrity who hovered behind him. He tapped the microphone belonging to a bargain bin karaoke system and quieted the crowd while Farnsworth and Diego meandered through the tightly packed bodies.

Farnsworth recognized him from the convention circuit.

"Greetings, fellow fans," he jokingly flashed a Vulcan hand gesture. "My name is Casey Kubrick—in addition to owning the well-known Goblin Hole, I am also a film director. I wanted to thank you so much for your support of the *Knights of the Illuvian Age*—as some of you might have heard, we're making a little movie about it."

A chorus of cheers rippled up from the crowd. Kubrick basked in their worship.

"Thank you. And thank *you* for helping make us the fastest *and* highest grossing Kickfunder campaign in the history of their crowd-funding platform!"

Another round of nasally adulation arose as Farnsworth grabbed Diego's arm. "That's what I was trying to tell you about. I think it's all connected."

Diego gave him a moment, but then whirled when something else caught his attention. "Got him."

The big man began picking his way through the room. Only after Farnsworth stood on his tip toes could he see their target. Henry Sheen milled near the platform where Kubrick stood with Wil Wheaton; his hands were in his pockets.

A horrific thought flashed through his mind. *Nobody knows what Zmei looks like. Maybe Sheen* is *Houdek—maybe he's here to kill Wheaton!*

He followed hot on Diego's heels as the mountain parted the crowd. His thoughts didn't add up, he knew—Sheen had been marked as a target, and Houdek had killed people while Sheen served time... but maybe it was all part of some grand misdirection?

Their path brought them close to the purchase register where Newt struggled to hang a flyer advertising twenty-percent off purchases during Wheaton's appearance.

Newt did a double-take when they passed and picked up his cellphone. He punched the keys like a nervous mole rat.

Farnsworth glanced back just as Newt dropped the mobile device. A text tone on the far side of the room caught his attention and he whirled back.

Sheen looked up from his phone and right at Diego. With a startled look on his face like a spooked deer, the ex-con turned and fled out the back door.

Diego pushed through the last few people between him and the exit. He darted in through the door and after his prey.

Few people paid any attention to the jostling near the fringes of the packed house. "And now," Kubrick stated, "for a man who needs no introduction in this crowd." He handed Wheaton the microphone as the audience applauded.

Farnsworth bullied his way back towards the register, his eyes locked firmly on Newt who stood straight and stiff like his genetics might be more fainting-sheep than man. The new detective put on a scowl every bit as menacing as he imagined his partner might wear.

Diego sprinted through the alleyway. He heard the screech of tires and knew that Sheen had gotten away—probably stolen a car since the criminal had arrived on foot. Slowing for a second, knowing he wouldn't ever catch him, the sudden fear that Sheen might've stolen *his car* launched him back into motion. He sprinted to the end of the alley and breathed a sigh of relief when he saw his Charger parked where he'd left it.

Ignoring the meter maid who tucked a parking ticket beneath his windshield wiper, Diego turned and dashed back to the front entrance of Comics Land. Pushing his way back through the crowd that had swelled and spilled into the sidewalk, he spotted his partner who had cornered the register jockey.

Farnsworth grabbed Newt's arm and wrested the phone away from him. He tapped the screen and the active window lit up showing Newt had texted a phone number—one he'd never traded previous messages with before—with a simple statement: *po po.*

Diego smiled as his partner wrapped his acquaintance's arm around his back and clapped a pair of cuffs on him.

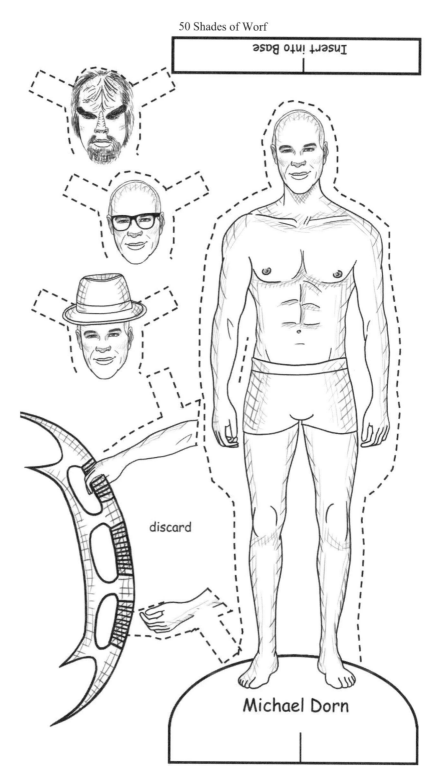

Insert into Base

discard

Michael Dorn

Post pics of your weirdest scenes to
#50ShadesofWorf

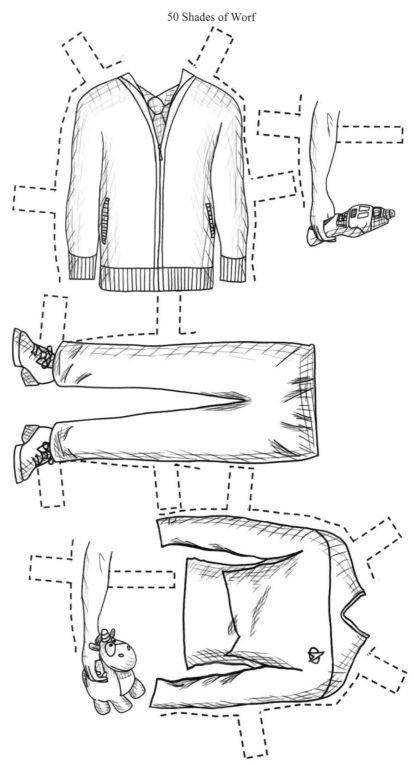

Post pics of your weirdest scenes to
#50ShadesofWorf

# PART THREE

## LAW & ORDER: COMICON DIVISION

# 22

Black Canary

Newt sat in handcuffs and bellied up to the table in the interrogation room. His bleary eyes and flushed cheeks clearly indicated he hadn't foreseen incarceration as a possible outcome of his actions.

The door swung open and the muscular Detective Rick Diego walked in wearing a face that indicated anything but pleasure. Moses Farnsworth, a butterball turkey by comparison, trailed after him with a stack of files.

"I haven't done anything wrong," Newt blurted out. He turned to Farnsworth. "You know me, Moses, tell him!"

Farnsworth only shrugged. "I guess I only *thought* I knew who *you* were, but these files say you're mixed up in some crazy stuff. I guess I *don't* really know you. *This guy...*" he nodded to the stack of manila folders, "*this guy probably even liked the Green Lantern movie.*"

Newt's face fell, crestfallen at such an accusation.

Diego raised an eyebrow, but pretended he knew what that all meant.

"When can I go?" Newt suddenly tried to act tough. "You don't have me tied to any crimes. I know, because I haven't committed any."

Sliding in close, Diego took a seat and one by one he removed crime scene photos related to the different crimes. "Drug running. Killing a bunch of mob enforcers. Money laundering. And then this one." He slid out a photo of Jared McCloud and the yellow-painted machinery at his murder scene. "First degree murder of a cop."

Farnsworth looked into Newt's bewildered face. "That last guy was a friend of mine."

With a mixture of awe and disgust Newt picked up the crime scene photo. "It's just like the *Caped Defenders* murder." He looked back up in shock, as if the pieces suddenly came together for him. "This is why you came into my shop the other day?"

They nodded.

"Okay. Okay. I'm cooperating. I'm not mixed up in any of this stuff—I just sent a text. The guy was supposed to help me with a few things but made me promise to text him if I saw any cops."

"Help you with what?"

Newt looked away, searching for an answer that might suffice... anything other than the real one.

Diego leaned forward imposingly. He growled, "Help *with what?*"

The weasel faced comic jockey broke down. "Listen, I really don't know much about him except that he's been to the shop a few times. He promised he could get some women who would help me film my Throne of Swords fan film."

Diego cocked his head and Farnsworth explained for his partner who was suddenly the naive one. "The kind of girls who don't like cops, ask to be paid up front, and are willing to do... that sort of stuff... on camera," He made an obscene hand gesture. "Swords may be figurative in this context."

Defeated, Newt sat there. He couldn't deny it and so he simply shrugged.

Diego's face scrunched slightly with disgust. "Has Henry Sheen been to the Goblin Hole?"

Newt shook his head yes. "None of that movie stuff ever happened, so I'm innocent, right? You can just track his phone and you have to let me go?"

With Newt finally cooperating, Farnsworth took a seat, too. "It was just a burner phone and he tossed it in the alleyway during the getaway."

Diego took another envelope and took out some sheets. "And you're not so innocent, CookieMonster_66," he called him by his online handle. He pointed at Farnsworth. "While I'm good at punching bad guys in the face, he's pretty good with the computer stuff. Tell me, do you know what the maximum pledge amount is for a Kickfunder contribution?"

Newt squeezed his lips together and played dumb.

"Twenty million dollars," Farnsworth said. "Not that those sorts of donations come in regularly, but the *Knights of the Illuvian Age* broke all sorts of records by raising enough capital to make a three hundred million dollar film budget. On a one hundred million dollar Kickfunder, they raised their minimum budget within five minutes—between just five donations. Twenty million apiece. Funny thing is, there sure wasn't much given away as far as backer goals for that level."

Newt gulped as Diego scanned him like a predator sizing up his prey. "Where the heck does a comic book store manager get that kind of cash?" He slid a page across the table showing a donation made at the Ultra Platinum Rainbow Bridge level contributed by CookieMonster_66. He slid a second one across that showed James Lee Anderson had also made one.

"That kind of timing," Farnsworth noted, "that's not a coincidence. That's a coordinated effort. Someone gave you the cash."

Newt gulped. "Yeah." His voice warbled. "Kubrick said he had some anonymous investors who wanted in—but needed to stay anonymous. He was planning to finance the rest out of pocket... money left over from the Stanley Kubrick Estate. I guess Casey grew up as a teen with the famous, reclusive director. This was gonna be Casey's magnum opus; I think he fancies himself the next Peter Jackson."

"Well, IMDB has never heard of him. Has ever directed anything else... besides the...uh, special kind of movies *you* were trying to make?" Diego clarified.

Newt shrugged with a frown.

"I just have some doubts that all of Kubrick's story is true. That money he got you to invest is blood money." Diego slid a new photo to him. A knifed body with a bad mullet. "Your buddy James Lee isn't going to see this film get made."

Farnsworth summarized the story for him. "Henry Sheen stole all that money from the Bratva—the Russian mob. They don't just want it back, they've sent a hit-man to kill everyone connected to their missing money... and if *we've* figured out where it went, certainly *they have too.*"

Newt began crying. "It was Sheen. Maybe he's a huge *Illuvian* fan or something. I'm not sure. I don't know all that much about it... or him. But Kubrick knows he offered up the cash for us to put in the fundraiser—he gave us each our pick of anything in the Goblin Hole if we played along." He sighed. "I got a mint All Star Comics number eight."

"First appearance of Wonder Woman? Niiiiice." Farnsworth almost sounded enthusiastic. He explained to Diego who shot him a look, "It's worth at least a hundred grand if it really is mint."

Lowering his head down to the table in shame Newt wearily confessed, "Yeah. I have a thing for Wonder Women. I already have a bunch of costumes."

Diego looked at him with a measure of disgust.

"Where those for yourself or the 'actors' you were buying for your film."

Newt began to sob with a wet, snotty cry. The answer may have been *both.*

"Well look who's a goblin hole, now?" Diego dropped as an insult. He looked to Farnsworth to see if the insult was valid. His nerdy partner gave him an approving nod. Newt just sobbed all the harder and mumbled something about a lawyer between ugly, tear-filled gasps.

Someone knocked on the door. Both detectives turned to look.

Captain Murphy stuck her head in and summoned them with a finger. "Detectives... a word?"

# 23

Murphy's Law

Farnsworth still held the stack of information he and Miles had ferreted out from the Internet. His boss looked at the sheaf of printouts.

"I'm sure that this information is all very useful. *My* question is if it's legal to have that in your possession," Murphy asked.

Farnsworth stiffened like someone had just shot a cold blast of wind up his rear.

"We'll make sure to file for a subpoena and get it right away." Diego shot Farnsworth a stern glare as his superior officer, but the twinkle in his eye seemed to glimmer with approval at finding the lead.

Murphy changed gears. "Chief Cooper gave me explicit instructions to make sure that Wil Wheaton was protected at all costs." Despite her short stature, Captain Murphy somehow managed to look down her nose at them. "We've got word now that Hit-man Houdek has already eliminated a couple targets. If you two haven't managed to find McCloud's killer by now, it'll be a wonder if Zmei doesn't beat you to his final target... this Wil Wheaton guy." Something in her tone hinted at a suggestion.

Bewildered, Farnsworth addressed the Captain. "Are you saying that you want us to hold off from investigating McCloud's killer?"

Murphy gave him a funny look, but Diego seemed capable of interpreting it. She reiterated, "The chief gave instructions to keep Wil Wheaton protected, but he didn't tell me how to do it."

Diego nudged Farnsworth. He pulled him aside and spoke in a hushed tone to give Murphy plausible deniability. "She knows it's all connected, just like the mob does. She's suggesting we use Wheaton as bait and get to the bottom of it. Best case scenario is that we catch Houdek."

"So what are we looking at, then?" The tone of Murphy's voice suggested that she wanted them to talk plainly.

"I think there's some kind of connection between Kubrick and Sheen," Diego stated.

Farnsworth nodded and took out his yellow legal pad with all of the prices of comics sold by Kubrick's Goblin Hole. "These are the last few prices of the major comics the Goblin Hole sold in the last several months."

Diego's eyebrows rose. "Those are some outrageous prices."

"I know," Farnsworth guffawed. "Most of these are only around half the value for their condition. But here's the thing: I don't have any records of where these comics came from."

"Counterfeit? Maybe a box in the attic?"

"No. The condition is too high for so many rare issues and high end collectors don't fall for fakes. I think there's more to Kubrick than he lets on, and I agree—he's connected to Sheen somehow. Maybe Sheen steals them for him? I don't know yet. I only know that the Goblin Hole has never had to buy new stock even though they've been around for as long as I can remember."

Diego paused for thought. "If Kubrick is shady too, and Sheen is tied to him, then this whole thing is probably much bigger than it looks at first glance. You think the actor is part of it too?"

Farnsworth shook his head. "Doubtful. Especially since he volunteered to give a huge chunk of his proceeds from the film to a charity."

The Captain waved her hands to keep them from veering off into the weeds. "Look, I don't know much about this Wheaton character; all I know is that Police Chief Cooper's son is a big fan. I don't really care about all that—but we got a killer lose in my city and I want him stopped."

She fixed her team with steely eyes. Every day some new twist in the case developed. "Quast!" she hollered for the woman who seemed best equipped to execute her orders. "I want to get surveillance on this Kubrick guy. If Sheen is trying to contact him, we need to know."

# 24

The List

"We need a list of everybody you think might be connected in some way to this thing," Farnsworth said as he slid a pen and paper across the table. "We don't want anybody else turning up like James Lee."

Newt began to write feverishly. The completed list included the top donors from the Kickfunder campaign, Wil Wheaton, Henry Sheen, and Casey Kubrick. A number of other names including Michael Dorn, William Shatner, and Kevin Sorbo filled out the list below, mainly unverified casting rumors from the internet bulletin boards. He pushed the paper across the table. "Okay. That's all I can really think of. What's next?"

Diego glared at him. "Now we put you in witness protection and hope that Bratva's assassins don't find you."

He looked like he wanted to argue, but Newt finally sat back defeatedly. If the mob thought he had helped, he was as good as dead.

"Officer Quast will be in shortly to give you the details, but your life is about to become very different," Diego said. "If you don't participate, however, the Bratva *will kill you*. You can not contact anyone or they'll find you." He stuck out his hand and beckoned for the man's cell phone.

Newt nodded slowly and put his device into Diego's palm.

Farnsworth took the paper and exited the interrogation room with his partner. "Who do we talk to first?"

Diego waved the phone. "If we pull some contacts off of here, do you suppose your buddy Miles can get a location for us?"

"Sheen ditched his phone, though."

"This goes beyond Sheen; even if he *was* the real killer, we haven't done justice to McCloud unless we take down every scumbag affiliated with whatever this mob-related mess really is."

"I'm sure Miles can find what you're looking for."

"Good," he said as he led the way towards the elevator. "You just follow my lead when we find the guy." Diego scanned the list and put a line through Sheen's name. "We know this guy is involved. The rest might or might not be guilty of anything more than being stupid, but I've got my suspicions."

Farnsworth scribbled out the other celebrity names that he knew from his browsing history weren't actually involved.

Diego circled the other four names on the list of major Kickfunder donors. "Have some squad-cars sent to each of these guys. Bring them all in. Also, get Quast to dig behind the scenes for any info on who Sheen spent time with in prison."

"What about Wheaton and Kubrick?"

"They'll get personal visits." Diego punched the elevator button and descended towards the dungeon.

# 25

Cardboard Castle

"Your buddy Miles is a fount of information," Diego said as he steered through traffic and took an exit for the convention center.

"He knows his stuff."

Diego slowed and parked his car in front of the main entrance where local staff had begun to hang signage for the con-goers they expected to attend TrollCON within the next couple days.

Farnsworth took the lead inside the building and picked up a flyer with a map of events and locations.

"You've been here before?" Diego asked.

"This convention? Yeah, lots of times, and a bunch of smaller ones, too."

The big man followed him through the halls which led to a huge room where a stage was partially constructed for the big event. "I supposed you already have your ticket for this one?"

Farnsworth's cheeks reddened. "I wasn't planning on attending this year," he said with a cagey tone. He pointed into the main arena, "There it is, the *Knights of the Illuvian Age* display."

Across the way, near the stage, the mountains of cardboard print material from beneath the Comics Land store had been constructed into a life-sized display. Adjacent to that, a sign hung across some partially erected shelves indicating the spot for The Goblin Hole Comics & Rarities.

Casey Kubrick, who they recognized from the earlier incident at Comics Land, fumbled with the racks as they approached. Farnsworth hung back, as directed, and let his partner handle the interviews.

"Mister Kubrick?" Diego flashed his badge.

He looked up, caught sight of the badge and then the face. He muttered an apology and said something about his helpers not showing up. He kept his face as neutral as if he'd been on the World Poker Tour.

"I hoped to ask you a few questions about Jim Newton?"

Kubrick stepped out of the nest of display units and vinyl signage. "How can I help you?"

"You are the owner of the Goblin Hole?" Diego kept going when Kubrick nodded. "I'm just doing a little investigating. There was a potential threat against a friend of yours. Do you know Jim Newton? He goes by Newt."

"I know him. He was supposed to help me with the setup today, along with some others, but mutual friends said he was arrested this morning and the others all bailed on me, so I'm a little busy right now."

Diego nodded. "Yeah. Well, Newt was into some weird stuff. He'll be going away for a while for it, but that's not our biggest concern. Someone threatened Newt," he lied. "Same kind of threat someone left for Wil Wheaton, who I think you also know."

Kubrick looked shocked. "Well I hope you catch this person."

"I think I know who it is," Diego said. "You don't happen to know Henry Sheen, do you?"

"I don't think so. I suppose I may have sold him a comic before. I don't remember every sale or the names of everyone I meet at these things."

"Right," Diego said suspiciously. "You sell pretty high end stuff, don't you?"

Kubrick nodded.

"How did you get started?"

"I started reselling comics about a decade ago. I found a big box of old comics in my attic and that pretty much set me up."

"Uh-huh. Pretty amazing story... you found millions of dollars' worth of comics in your attic. Where do you resupply from now — do you go to auctions?"

"It was a big box," Kubrick narrowed his eyes. "If you'll excuse me, I have a lot of setup to do and fewer hands, now."

Diego grinned, recognizing that he'd struck a sore spot. "I'd certainly hate to hold you up. If you can think of anything we ought to know about Henry Sheen please don't wait to call. He's a very dangerous individual—especially to you, if he's threatening your big celebrity." He angled his head towards a life-sized cardboard cut-out of Wheaton.

"If anything comes up I'll let you know."

Diego nodded and left with Farnsworth in his shadow.

Several paces away Diego glanced back over his shoulder and scowled.

"What are you thinking?"

"He pretended like it was no big deal, but I could see it in his eyes... the intentional indifference... that was not the first time Casey Kubrick has laid eyes on me."

Farnsworth shot a look behind them, too. "What does that mean? Maybe he saw you at Comics Land when we arrested Newt?"

"I don't know... yet."

# 26

Bologna Screams

"You didn't tell Kubrick that an assassin wants to kill him," Farnsworth observed as they left the building and headed for the hotel.

"I didn't think he needed to know just yet," Diego said. "But if the Bratva is chasing an actor, they'll certainly come after the director, too."

Farnsworth guessed, "He doesn't know about it yet, that's why you blamed Wheaton's threat on Sheen?"

"Now you're catching on, kid. And Sheen might not know about Houdek yet, either. I suppose if Houdek catches up with him before we do it's just sweet justice… that's why we've got to get those other donors into protection as soon as possible. We don't want anyone to flee town before we've got it all figured out."

They rode a few more moments in silence. "You're not going to tell Wheaton either, are you?"

"We can't. And as long as we can keep an eye on him, we'll be sure to cross paths with Zmei."

"You know, Chief Cooper will be ticked if something happens to him. Like *really mad*."

"Yeah," Diego muttered. "I heard something about his kid being a big fan."

Farnsworth bit his lip. "That's not exactly the truth." He opened a file folder and took out a print up revealing the true names and personal information of all the Kickfunder backers. "Chief Cooper is the fan. His son could care less."

"Kids use their parent's accounts all the time for stuff like this," Diego started.

Farnsworth shook his head. He took out a few prints and smiled with tight lips. "You might say the Chief is something of a Wesley Crusher." He tapped his heart.

"I don't know what that means."

He handed the photos over as he explained. "He's got a very hi-tech security system in his house... one with wi-fi remote access. The kind of thing guys like Miles can exploit."

Diego guffawed when he recognized the man sitting on a couch while wearing a Star Trek uniform. Chief Cooper's private man cave was set up like a starship bridge; science fiction memorabilia adorned the walls.

The big detective cringed. "I'm not sure I wanted to know that."

"I think it demonstrates exactly how important this is to the chief. Wil Wheaton was part of the original cast of one of his favorite shows," he explained.

A light bulb seemed to go off behind Diego's eyes. "Well hopefully this whole convention business is over soon and we'll get everything wrapped up before all is said and done."

Farnsworth said nothing. He knew Diego wouldn't let up until McCloud's murder was solved.

After a short car ride the detectives found themselves at Wheaton's hotel door. The elevator doors parted and they heard screaming as it echoed down the hallway. Diego drew his gun and hurried through the corridor. Farnsworth copied his movements.

Rounding a corner they found two uniformed officers sitting outside the door where the shrieks were coming from. The two guards looked bewildered but said nothing.

Diego pounded on the door with a clenched fist. "Wil Wheaton? Mr. Wheaton, are you okay? I'm gonna bust this door down!" He tensed his body, ready for action, when everything went silent. The door opened.

Wil Wheaton wore only an untied bathrobe as he opened the door. "Oh, hello." He looked down his nose at the two guards outside. "Guys. I thought I said I didn't want to be disturbed." He shrugged, "Oh well. Right this way," he ushered them into his suite and cracked a handful of pistachio nuts.

The tall detective couldn't mask the confusion on his face.

Wheaton explained, "I'm doing some voice over work that requires a lot of screaming. Gotta keep the pipes in practice."

Farnsworth hadn't retained a scrap of the earlier weirdness. He pursed his lips and moved anxiously, like a toddler who had to pee. "It's an honor to meet you Mister Wheaton."

Diego glared at him, hoping he'd settle down. "We're just here to ask you a few questions, Mister Wheaton."

"Please, just call me Wil."

Farnsworth peeped with an awkward kind of hum at the notion, but held his tongue.

"Do you happen to know this man?" Diego held up a photo of Henry Sheen.

"No. Is he the man who stabbed my door?"

Diego didn't answer. He held up a new photo of Newt. "How about him?"

Wheaton shook his head.

He held a third one. Casey Kubrick.

"Yeah. I know that one. Wait—you think that weird director guy did it?"

"No, no." Diego stated. "But since we're on the subject, how long have you known him?"

"We hadn't really met until I agreed to do *Knights of the Illuvian Age*. He'd contacted my agent and we did a lot on faith since he made sure everything was paid. There isn't even a solid contract yet; we won't have that until the Kickfunder is concluded in..." he looked at his naked wrist, "a little under a week."

"Do you think anyone would want to hurt you or scare you?"

Wheaton looked at the big detective with a serious face. "Michael Dorn."

Diego furrowed his brow but Farnsworth's jaw dropped. "Not Michael Dorn!"

"Afraid so. There's been something of a feud happening at any convention we've both been guests at. I mean, two years ago at a dinner party his cat, Gowron, knocked up my Princess McMittens at a Star Trek reunion event and he's flat out refused pay kitten support. *Then*, we got involved in this DDR arcade challenge and I spilled a whole bunch of soda on the machine..."

"And it shorted out before he could beat your high score?" interjected Farnsworth.

"No. He totally destroyed me. But *then* he slipped on the dance pad and hit his head. And *then* it shorted out and zapped him pretty good... it burned a hole right through the cheeks of his pants." He tilted his head back and laughed. "It was amazing. But yeah, I've been on his bad side ever since."

Diego's phone buzzed with a text from Quast.

"Do you think I'm in danger?" Wheaton asked.

"No. We think it was just someone trying to prank you," Diego said and then indicated to Farnsworth that he needed to make a quick call. He turned and spoke in hushed tones, several paces away.

"So..." Farnsworth tried to stall. "You're a big *Knights of the Illuvian Age* fan?"

"Of course."

"Do they have a screenplay yet? Have you seen it?"

A mischievous glimmer twinkled in Wheaton's eye. "You're wondering how they plan to handle the unicorn sex scene?"

Farnsworth blushed and shrugged.

"I haven't seen the full script yet. But I've been told ye old pokey horse is a significant part of the special effects budget."

Diego was still on the phone and couldn't help the new detective.

"I had your action figure when I was a kid," Farnsworth blurted out.

Wheaton raised an eyebrow. "You ever make me do anything weird?"

"Of course…"

"Well now it's my turn."

"Wha…"

"Turn about's fair play. Now you have to do what I tell you—it's only fair. Stand on one leg."

Farnsworth inexplicably obeyed.

Wheaton took a jar of peanuts from the cupboard. "Are you allergic to peanuts?"

Farnsworth shook his head.

Wheaton grimaced and put them back, instead turning to the mini-fridge. "Okay. Well I think I have some questionable bologna in here I can make you eat."

Diego hung up and rescued Farnsworth. "We've got to go. Thank you, Mister Wheaton, for your time."

The two left and walked down the hall towards the elevator. Diego rolled his eyes and muttered, "Celebrities," just as the screaming resumed.

As soon as the elevator doors closed he told Farnsworth the news. "All of the other big-donors for the Kickfunder are dead already. The killer left behind a butterfly knife at each scene."

# 27

Tycho

The hands on the clock had tipped hard left as Farnsworth pulled up a stool near Diego's desk. The plain steel workstation had all the character of unsalted nursing-home food. He raised an eyebrow as Diego plopped into his chair.

He defended, "What? We can't all work in Disneyland, ya know."

Farnsworth shrugged and then blushed as Jenny Quast approached, right on schedule. Her face remained perfectly placid as she moved towards them in her signature gait.

She handed over a stack of files with the details from the newest four murders. They were all largely the same: relatively isolated and lonely comic book junkies found dead amongst their stacks of collectible memorabilia.

If Newt hadn't been arrested for sending that text, he would've been dead, too.

"I have been able to interview one of the two cellmates Henry Sheen had during prison," she said. "Jake Tycho is still incarcerated and so I sat down with him. The other one, Danny Di Santo, is harder to locate. His PO was transferred a year ago so Di Santo has been difficult to keep tabs on since. I've got local guys looking for him."

"What does Tycho have to say?"

"He gave me the backstory about what went down. Sheen had initially cut a deal when he got pinched the first time by

McCloud. He'd hidden a big stash of drug money and was supposed to rat out the high members of the Bratva under oath, before going into witness protection. On the stand, he suddenly changed his mind and only gave up a few low-level guys; most of them were already dead or in prison."

"Let me guess," said Diego, "he kept the money and did the time?"

Quast nodded. It was maybe the most Diego had ever seen her head move. "That explains why he could get a job for the mob again. He never really left. He just took a two million dollar payoff and kept his mouth shut."

The feet on Farnsworth's stool creaked as he leaned. "I don't know. He didn't seem very well-off when we first met him at the corner store. Sheen really seemed like he needed that job. Where did all that money go?"

"Not everybody is addicted to Batman. He probably blew it on drugs and hookers."

Farnsworth shrugged, but his expression indicated he still had his doubts.

"I'll keep searching for Di Santo," Quast said. She spotted Captain Murphy's approach and ducked away.

"Farnsworth. A word?" Murphy asked.

Diego glanced at the clock and grabbed his jacket. He gave them both a curt nod, twirled his keys on his fingers, and departed. It was late and the bad guys could wait until morning.

Farnsworth stood nervously and followed the Captain to her lair.

"I just wanted to tell you that you're doing well so far. Usually by this time in the week Diego and McCloud have blown up a building or had a high speed chase. Anyway, I need you to do me a favor... something that lines up with your expertise."

# 28

Plan B

Moses Farnsworth slipped inside the home he shared with his mother and hurried through the kitchen before she could engage him in conversation. The broken plate still laid on the gold-flecks and mint formica countertop as an everlasting testament to Ethel Farnsworth's dissatisfaction.

He slipped around the corner and got to the basement stairs before she could shuffle into the hall.

"Moses? Moses! What about the squirrel? Did you get to the gutters?"

"Not now, Ma—I've got a lot on my plate," he called over his shoulder as he descended the final steps.

"Moses get back here. I don't do stairs anymore and I can't talk to you while you're down there."

"I'm fine with that arrangement," he said.

"Well! I never..."

Moses closed the door to his room and shut her out. He flopped onto his bed and ground his teeth while his stomach flipped and turned in knots. Farnsworth rolled over onto his back and stared at his old poster. An autographed movie poster from the theatrical release of Robocop hung by a wad of long-since-hardened rubber adhesive. "Don't look at me like that," he groaned.

His inner fears and demons wreaked havoc on his nerves.

Captain Murphy had asked him for a simple favor—something that he just couldn't do. She'd offered him everything that he'd always wanted, but he'd suddenly faltered and fallen into a pit of his own insecurities.

He hung his head again and screamed into his pillow. Finally, he sat up, sure that he'd give himself an ulcer at this rate.

Farnsworth grimaced and picked up an information packet that his mother had left out for him. The brochure read *The joys of being an insurance salesman.*

# 29

Dork Infested Waters Without a Paddle

Diego walked into the precinct and stifled a yawn.

Murphy watched him over the top of her coffee mug like a predatory animal. "Diego!"

He whirled around and spotted her rumbling towards him as if he'd just stolen an idol made of South American gold. Diego blinked, unsure what had her so riled up this early in the morning.

She spat accusingly, "What did you say to Farnsworth?"

"Um, what? I'm not sure what you're talking about."

"Last night after I spoke with him he asked to be put back on regular duty after giving him his dream job: going under cover with you at this stupid, upcoming TrollCON thing."

Diego grimaced and thought it over. He couldn't come up with an explanation. The first day had been rocky, but he thought that yesterday had gone smoothly. Shrugging, he said, "I don't know. Maybe he just felt like he couldn't do the job."

She scowled. "Can't do the job? *Please.* The Chief says this is one of the biggest four conventions in this corner of the country. Guys like Farnsworth live for this kind of stuff."

"Let me talk to him. I'll get to the bottom of it..."

"Good luck. Whatever's bothering him has got him so twisted up that he called in sick today." She slapped a book into his hands.

"What's this?" He turned it over and read the cover. *How to Speak Geek and Influence Nerds*.

"You better read that if you can't get him back on board. You're going to need some kind of guide through dork-infested waters without your partner. Remember, if anything happens to that actor, Cooper will can your sorry behind."

Diego inhaled a sharp breath. He opened the cover to a page showing Spiderman and his uncle Ben and read a few lines. The detective used the book to salute the captain, and then grabbed his keys.

Heading for the exit, he stopped Jenny Quast. "Hey. Do you happen to know where Moses Farnsworth lives?"

Without hesitation she rattled of his address.

He glanced sideways at her but figured maybe she had a photographic memory. "Um. Right. Can you text that to me?"

She handed him a piece of paper. "Write your number down."

"Just yesterday you texted me with… nevermind." He jotted his digits and walked to his car.

The text arrived while he hit the freeway. After a short drive Diego found himself parking in front of an unassuming bungalow in an aging residential section on the city's outskirts. A mid-80s Yugo sat parked in the driveway, though it looked as if it had been sometime since it had moved.

A polite, aged woman named Ethel Farnsworth met him at the door. "Oh my. Aren't you a big fella?" She thumped him on the chest for good measure.

"Yes Ma'am. Is Moses here?"

"Right this way." She adjusted her coke bottle glasses and led him through the house. She shuffled along at a brisk pace for someone with a walker… but she did not have a walker. Her fuzzy slippers slapped *thak thak* against the bottoms of her feet like flip flops.

One entire wall was adorned floor to ceiling with decorative plates; another was covered with awkward-family-style photos of Ethel posed with various cats throughout the years. Only two photos of Moses made the wall. There appeared to be no Mr. Farnsworth.

"It's about time some of Moses's work friends dropped by," Ethel paused at the top of the steps and motioned for him to descend. "I'm sorry, but Moses has made it quite clear that the basement is his personal space. Besides, I don't trust myself on the stairs, anyways," she said in a contrived, saintly tone.

"Thank you Ma'am."

"I'll make you boys some Hot Pockets and Kool-aid for when you come up. Do you like Strawberry Blast or purple?"

"Oh. No thanks. I'm just here too..."

She didn't seem to understand the word "no."

"You know what," Diego said, "purple would be just fine."

Ethel smiled and turned back to the kitchen while Rick Diego began his slow descent on the narrow, carpeted stairs.

# 30

The Basement

Moses Farnsworth looked up when someone knocked at his door. He opened it to find Diego hunched to avoid bumping his head on the slightly lower-than-code ceilings. Farnsworth sighed, "What do you want?"

From within the hallway of the basement Diego looked around nervously. Three rooms and a living room split off of what appeared to be an older apartment-style addition to the home. Each one seemed well-stocked with collectible items and comic book paraphernalia. He ducked into Farnsworth's room. "Murphy said you were bailing on this case—and on the promotion." Diego stared at him, expecting an answer.

Farnsworth merely shrugged and refused to meet his gaze.

"Listen, if it's something that I said or did..." Diego looked around what was clearly Farnsworth's bedroom. The shorter detective assured Diego that he had nothing to do with it.

"You were right. I'm just not cut out for this. I'd do terrible justice to McCloud's memory. I dunno... maybe I'll sell insurance or something like my mom says."

The mention of his dead partner made Diego bristle. Something deep inside of Diego insisted that he needed Farnsworth's help in order to catch the killer. He felt lost enough inside Comics Land; he would be a total wreck without a guide at TrollCON.

His eyes caught a few movie posters. An over-sized print of Detective Comics number twenty-seven featured an airborne Batman; near that, Stallone's jawline protruded from a Judge Dredd banner. Near the door hung the theatrical poster for the first Robocop film.

Diego looked closer where an encouraging sticky note was posted above his bed: Farnsworth was drawn like a hero in Quast's unmistakable style hung near the cyborg policeman near another of her notes with a caricature of Samuel L Jackson saying "Bad MF-er."

"How long have you wanted to be a cop?"

"Pretty much all my life," Farnsworth perked up.

"And how many of these comic convention things have you been to before?"

"A lot... several per year, actually. I've got a whole room dedicated to costuming," he motioned towards his craft room down the hall.

"And you've been to TrollCON..."

"I've gone the last ten years in a row."

A few lines he'd read from Murphy's book sprang to Diego's mind. "What's that thing that Uncle Ben is always telling Spiderman?"

"'With great power comes great responsibility?'"

"Exactly!" Diego said. "Right now you have a responsibility to help me. You're a walking guide to this subculture. I know nothing about it... and if we're going to catch Jared's killer, I need your help."

All the momentum Diego had built up came to a screeching halt.

"I... I can't." Farnsworth turned his face away.

"Did you get kicked out or something?" Not that Diego could imagine mild mannered Moses Farnsworth doing anything worthy of getting himself banned from the event center. "We'll be under cover. No one will ever know it's you."

Farnsworth looked optimistic for a second, and then shook his head.

"Come on! You've got to tell me *why* at least. You owe me that much."

"You're just going to laugh or say it's stupid."

Diego steeled his innards to make sure he wouldn't laugh, no matter how absurd it might be. "Try me. Tell me anyway. This is important—*it's for McCloud.*"

Farnsworth bit his lip and wiped the sweat from his palms. After several long seconds he broke. "Okay. Fine. I'll go. But I haven't been to a con in almost a year, now. Before, I never missed one; it's one of the great places where guys like me can really be who they were meant to be and hang out with... the people who I only see every couple months at conventions."

Diego narrowed his eyes as he put the pieces together in his mind. "What's her name?"

Farnsworth stiffened. He hadn't meant to be so easy to read. Wiping the embarrassment from his face he admitted, "Jessica."

Nodding to the sticky notes, Diego asked, "Has Quast ever been to one of these things with you?"

All the blood seemed to drain from Farnsworth's face at the notion. "She can never know about Jessica."

Diego almost laughed, but caught himself. "Jesus, man. It seems like she really did a number on you."

"I knew she wasn't the right girl for me... but she was *so forward* and I just couldn't say no. I... did something. She must be furious with me—I can't let her find me, and I'm sure she'll be there. She's always at these cons."

"Hey," Diego tried to console him. "I'm sure she can be dodged or avoided or whatever. Heck, if I have to, I'll just make something up and arrest her. It's that important that you get there. Lives literally hang in the balance. One very important life in particular."

Farnsworth exhaled a tense breath and stared at the ground. "Wil Wheaton."

The senior detective nodded. "You can either face your fear of this she-devil cosplay woman or Wil Wheaton dies. With all of the security Murphy has posted at the hotel, the convention center will be the obvious place for Houdek to strike."

He took a deep breath. "As long as you're sure Jessica won't be a problem..."

Diego clapped him on the back. "Deal. Now what are we gonna need to blend in at this thing?"

He took a look over Diego's impressive physique. "Costumes are always a big part of cons. How comfortable are you with partial nudity?"

# 31

Kinkos

Diego knocked on the door to the chief's office.

"You'd better have good news for me," she waved him in.

"Yeah. Farnsworth is back in. He's got something of an enemy that goes to these things, but I got it taken care of. He's back on board now and acting like a tiny little dictator." He rolled his eyes.

Murphy looked up at the taller man and scowled.

"No offense," he said as he dropped a few forms on her desk.

"What's this?" She scanned the requisition forms and her eyebrows raised. "You need *how much?*" She flipped the pages. "You need almost twelve thousand dollars? For comic books!"

Diego winced at the pitch of her voice, afraid she might break the windows or summon a horde of angry dogs.

"Not exactly. It's more like two thousand for supplies that..."

"I *see* that. You need ten grand in cash on top of it. Tell me you're not planning to finance some kind of action figure collection with this."

He handed her Farnsworth's map of the comic convention. Sharpie scribbles marked different locations on the map's layout.

"This mark right here is where Casey Kubrick, a key part of our investigation, will spend most of his time. We strongly believe Sheen was trying to contact Kubrick after he first fled and he's been under obvious surveillance, since. This other mark is where Wil Wheaton's celebrity table is for meet and greets, photos, and whatever else they do at these things."

"And this other mark down here?"

"Our best vantage point to keep an eye on both. We're going to need to get a vendor booth. This is a vendors-only row. These things normally have to be secured like six months ahead of time and cost about three grand..."

Murphy choked on her coffee. "To sell comic books and toys?"

Diego continued, "But we were able to bribe a guy to get us in even though all of the flyers have already been printed. As a vendor, we'll be able to get our weapons in through the loading gate and stash them under the table each night; they only do security screenings at the front."

The captain grimaced, but finally she nodded as she reviewed the requisitions list. In the end this was still cheaper than damages from the car chase Diego and McCloud were involved in two months ago. Murphy scanned the requisition details. "You guys sure plan to spend a lot of money on baby oil and body paint," she mused.

Diego rocked on his heels. "Not my idea. Farnsworth insists we go in costume."

"You know, you can't be a vendor if you don't have something to sell."

"I have an idea about that. It's all covered."

Murphy shot him a hesitant look but signed the forms and freed up the cash for them. "Good luck."

Diego wasn't sure how to respond. He had very little idea what might come next.

After a short search he found Jenny Quast. Preoccupied, she barely looked up from her workstation; they'd barely had any rapport over the years aside from strictly professional duties.

"I need to ask you a big favor."

She leaned back slightly, setting her work aside, and gave him her attention.

"I've noticed your artwork. You're really good at it."

"Do you spend a lot of time looking at art, Detective Diego?"

Diego blushed as if she'd called his bluff. "Well, I like art... yours anyway. I was hoping you could let me use some of it during an undercover operation at the..."

"No." She turned back to her work. "My actual pieces, the ones that are more than just doodles, they are deeply personal."

Diego explained that he needed something to sell at the vendor table at TrollCON and his partner had told him that a lot of artists sell prints at their tables.

She barely looked up at him, head unmoving, and then turned her eyes back to her work.

"It's for McCloud... and Farnsworth," he said. "This whole operation is his idea—his first big one."

She somehow managed to bite her lip and sigh without ever moving an eyebrow. "For Farnsworth?" Her cheeks flushed ever so slightly. "Give me a moment." A minute later she handed over a USB flash-drive filled with digital scans of her work.

"Thank you," he said. "And I really do like your art."

Diego turned and looked at the office printing machine. "I think I need to get to a Kinkos."

"You know they haven't called it that since before 2008, right?"

Diego shrugged and departed. He still had to print and laminate hundreds of graphics and buy a case of body paint.

# 32

Calm Before the Storm

Diego fidgeted with the costuming pieces Farnsworth draped over his body. He'd already explained the plan in detail. "Why can't we just go and sit in our booth like normal cops on a stake-out? I don't get why you insist on doing costumes."

"Because you have a cop look," Farnsworth said. "This will help hide it."

"Fine. But why go to such lengths?" He scanned the room. Custom, plastic molds and various costuming props and pieces littered the room.

"Because nothing sticks out worse at these things than a *bad* costume. With the really good ones people stop and take photos, but they usually pay more attention to the costume than the wearer. It's like hiding in plain sight."

Diego scowled.

"If you want to keep your cover so we can catch Henry Sheen, assuming he's gotten a new ticket, this is the best way. Remember, Sheen already knows what you look like."

The big man blew a raspberry and tried on the last costume pieces that Farnsworth wrapped him with. He didn't mind the biker gear, as long as it didn't take on a YMCA flair... especially given the details of how he'd managed to get them into the convention.

He flexed and moved in the getup. "This is it? It's not so bad, comparatively speaking."

Farnsworth chuckled. "Oh there's more, but we won't worry about that until tomorrow. Are you comfortable wearing contacts?"

Diego's brows knit together.

"Never mind. Don't worry about it now. We've got a lot to do in the morning."

Checking the clock, Diego replied, "Yeah. And I've still got to pick up all of those prints from Kinkos."

"What the heck is Kinkos?"

Diego tightened his jaw. "Tomorrow… be ready early."

Farnsworth nodded and smeared a dab of white goo on his partner's arm and cheek. "Don't wipe it off," he howled when Diego reached for a rag. "It's just a test strip to make sure you're not going to have an allergic reaction to the paint."

Diego looked worried, but took out his keys and sighed on his way out the door. He muttered, "This is how I live my life now…"

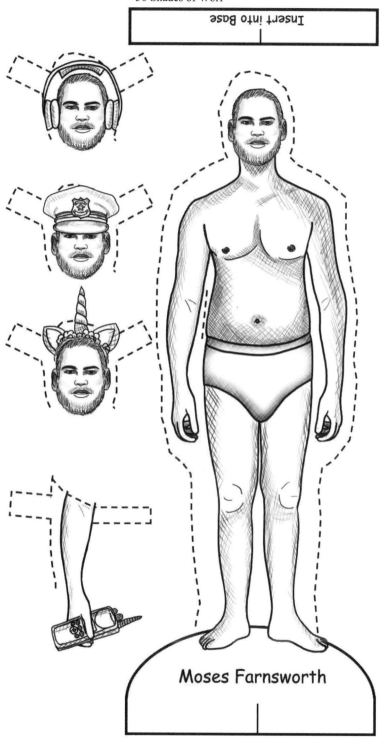

Insert into Base

Moses Farnsworth

Post pics of your weirdest scenes to
#50ShadesofWorf

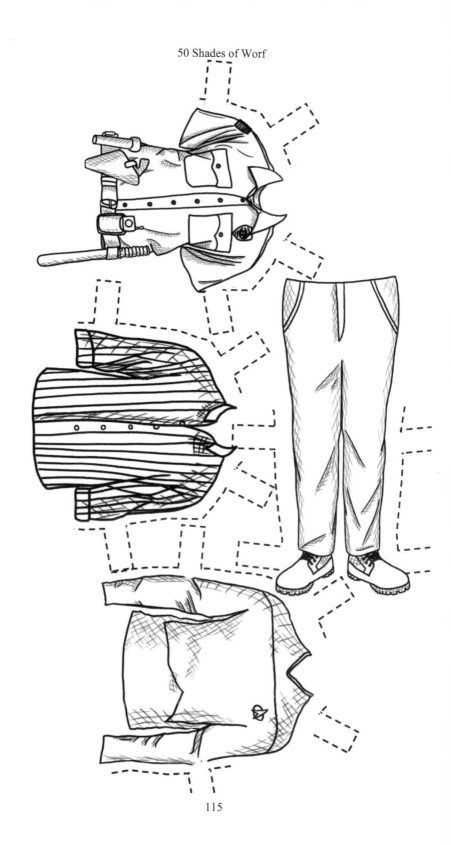

Post pics of your weirdest scenes to
#50ShadesofWorf

# PART FOUR

## DAY 1

# 33

Day 1

Traffic around the convention center was stop and go with the sudden increase in foot and vehicle traffic.

Farnsworth checked his watch and exhaled through his nose as they waited for a parade of motionless automobiles in front of them to recognize that the light had turned green. Only about three cars passed through every green light.

A beat up, decommissioned school bus took up nearly all the parking on one side of the street. Its side had been dressed with a twenty-foot banner covered with crosses and Judeo-Christian iconography. Big, hand-printed lettering read *Stop Sending Children too Hell!* The second o in the line had been painted over to try and match the background after someone realized the spelling error after the fact.

The sidewalk in front of the bus boasted a cluster of overweight, bearded men and women seated in lawn chairs. They held poorly crafted signs proclaiming a number of slogans, *D&D=BADD, Star Wars is Satanism, Imagination leads to Hell, CS Lewis Worships False gods,* and any number of other inflammatory statements.

Each one wore a general look of disinterest as they passed out evangelistic tracts to the passersby on the sidewalk. Mounds of tossed-aside pamphlets had piled up fifteen feet on either side of the protesters' zone.

A woman with straight hair that hung almost as low as the hem of her ankle-length jean skirt slid tracts off her stack like a rich kid making it rain on his eighteenth birthday, though her face had no such similar excitement. Six children between the ages of two and five hugged her leg as if afraid to be in public.

"What the heck?" Diego asked. "Is that the Westboro Baptist Church or something?"

"No," Farnsworth sighed watching a man wearing a sandwich board depicting a twisted, demonic looking Pikachu as it killed a child. He screamed something about Pokemon being dangerous to children's mental health. "It's the regular kind of Baptists... sort of. Every community seems to have a handful of nutters like these."

The man in the wearable sign stood next to a barbecue grill. With a zealous shout he threw a stuffed Squirtle on the fire and screamed, "Die Satan!" The flame retardant materials in the child's toy didn't flare up quite like expected and so the protester shot it with another dose of lighter fluid, sending a fireball three feet into the air.

"They show up every year, it seems like. Usually only to the big ones. They apparently 'care more about evangelism' when there's a possibility of media presence."

Diego pointed to a smaller huddle adjacent to the protesters. They looked identical, but the groups were obviously quarreling. All of the smaller team's signs called down curses upon the General Baptist convention. "Then who are *they*?"

"Those are the *Southern* Baptists." At the rear, two young men from opposing camps threw trash at each other like children, and a woman on each side shoved at each other like unpainted, denim Barbie dolls.

"Why don't they protest together, I mean, if you really had to protest at all?" Diego asked.

"They don't get along." Farnsworth simply left it at that.

Twenty feet away from the John-the-Baptist Glee Club and just beyond the pamphlet graveyard, a college kid stood holding a big box. His t-shirt read Durex and featured an 8-bit old man saying, "It's dangerous to go alone! Take this." The screen-printed shirt's arrow pointing down to a huge box of free prophylactics the man held. Much younger passersby greedily stuffed their pockets with hope and lusty optimism.

Apparently everyone from Jesus to Hugh Hefner's ghost saw the convention as an opportunity to market something.

The light finally turned green and the road cleared up enough to let them pass as far as the parking area.

# 34

Loading

Diego said nothing more as his car approached the loading dock at the back of the convention center. He could barely stand to look in his rear view mirror. Every time he glanced at himself he cringed deep inside.

The big detective tried to hide his frown and refused to look at his partner who wore a renaissance-like hood and cowl. He was supposed to be some character from *Knights of the Illuvian Age* with a name that Diego couldn't even pronounce.

He glanced at the clock and tightened his fists around the steering wheel. Luckily the artist partners that Diego bribed had already set their booth up. They only needed to hang Quast's prints to complete the set up.

The black Charger zoomed through the underground loading dock and braked to a halt at the loading bay. Farnsworth seemed to bounce with eagerness as they got closer. He'd called it con-fever, but Diego felt certain that all the energy drinks had something to do with it.

Before either could exit the vehicle, a security guard hurried over to the car. The rent-a-cop tapped the glass with his flashlight which made Diego bristle. He was very protective about his car.

Diego tensed and sucked in a breath as he grabbed the handle, about to exit and tear the ridiculous cop-mustache from the silly little man's face. He glanced over and caught the look of warning in Farnsworth's eyes; they seemed to say *don't blow our cover!*

Sighing, Diego relaxed his grip on the handle and instead rolled the window down.

"You can't park here," the guard said with smug tone.

"But we're vendors." Diego flashed him their vendor badges and parking permit.

The guard, whose name tag read Harding, shook his head like a peacock. "Not my problem," he quipped, drunk with the power his plastic badge and minimum wage provided him with. "You should've been here two hours ago. The dock is closed to vehicles. You still load in through here, but you've got to move this car to the lot and load in by hand."

Diego turned to better address him with a rational argument.

Harding raised his eyebrows as if he welcomed the challenge and whipped out his booklet of parking warnings. They weren't *tickets* and carried no monetary fine; Harding didn't have any real kind of power, but he brandished his feathers all the same.

With a squint and grind of his teeth, Diego peeled out of the lot and found one of the few remaining parking spots at the back of the designated zone. He cursed under his breath, knowing it would be a long walk and his crotch had already begun to sweat within the leather club pants. He didn't even want to know *why* Farnsworth owned a pair of them.

Farnsworth sprang from the front seat like a hungry kid about to enter Willy Wonka's factory. "Come on! We don't want to miss the opening rush."

Diego leaned into the backseat and grabbed the duffel bag filled with laminated art prints and other supplies they would need at their booth. His partner snatched their convention badges; Farnsworth had already warned him that if security spotted him without one he'd be quickly tossed from the grounds.

Looking up from his car he spotted a group of normal-looking business people on the sidewalk. A whole street full of people seemed to pass nearby on their way to work or the bus stop. All of them stopped and stared at the two costumed detectives who stood in the middle of the parking area like aliens from a distant planet.

Farnsworth skipped on ahead, oblivious, but Diego froze, suddenly as self-conscious as a teenage boy in sweat pants who'd just realized girls were attractive. He turned and walked briskly to catch up.

"I feel stupid and don't know why you made me dress up like Rob Zombie. A ballcap and aviator shades would've been the perfect cover."

"Pssh. Oh, relax and enjoy it. Once you're inside you'll fit in perfectly... unless you accidentally go through the wrong door and into the shoe-salesman's convention." He grimaced introspectively. "Never again," Farnsworth whispered.

"You are supposed to be Lobo. Just use the words I taught you and refer to yourself in the third person. Maybe cuss a lot, unless there are kids around." Farnsworth cycled through the list. "Bastich, fraggin everything, and call yourself the 'Main Man.'"

"I don't know what any of those things mean," he said and then muttered. "I'm going to sound so stupid."

"Just talk like Macho Man Randy Savage."

Diego worriedly curled a lip and shrugged.

"Seriously? You don't know Macho Man?"

"I think we had very different childhoods."

"He's the old Slim Jim guy!"

"Oh. Gotcha. *I can snap into a slim-Jim, ooh-yeah!*" Diego practiced. "I'm the Main Man!"

Farnsworth grinned. "You got it down."

Finally, they got through the loading dock. Harding waved at them and flashed a cocky smile as they walked buy.

"*Fraggin Bastich,*" Diego muttered.

# 35

Setup

The hooded Farnsworth had to practically drag Diego along. Everywhere, and from every angle, brightly colored and graphics-heavy advertisements grabbed the detectives' eyes.

Diego, a first-timer, suffered a mild stroke like a toddler visiting Chuck E Cheese. Farnsworth had to coax him along like a puppy. Whirling all around them costumed vendors and one very lost shoe salesman hurried to put the finishing touches on their displays. A barely comprehensible voice announced over the loudspeaker that the con would open to the public in ten minutes.

Shaking his head clear from the sensory overload, Diego spotted a giant print displaying the yellow, smiley faced piano crushing a beloved hero. He set his jaw and remembered the reason they'd come.

Freestanding signs stood posted at regular intervals. They read *Please use your best CONduct* and then listed simple, good human skills like healthy eating and basic hygiene practices. Diego wrinkled his nose. "My God… do these people actually need reminders to brush their teeth and wear deodorant?"

His partner shrugged. "You'd hope not. But by day three you'll begin to notice a… distinct odor."

They both grimaced and hurried along.

Arriving at the booth, Farnsworth shot his partner an awkward look. Diego began clipping prints to the rack behind the table, paying no attention to the sign that skirted the booth. *Mike & Jimmy: Partners in Art.* The bold, block lettering was overlaid with brilliant rainbow stripes. He chuckled; for all the senior detective's street-smarts and abilities, he seemed oblivious to certain aspects of cultures other than the hard-boiled underworld.

Diego worked like a dog; he pinned up poster-sized prints like a robot on a mission. His brain hadn't even registered the content of the artwork they were claiming to have created as part of their cover.

"What?" Diego groused as he took a seat and affixed their handguns beneath the table. The announcer began counting down from ten to announce the opening of the con.

Farnsworth merely pointed at Quast's creations. His jaw hung agape.

Diego turned around. His expression matched Farnsworth's. Of the thirty pieces hanging there, most of them were highly detailed depictions of officers from the precinct, each reimagined as pop art pieces in inappropriate or highly suggestive poses. Most subjects wore sci-fi or fantasy dress; many were part animal. All bordered on salacious.

"Whoah," Diego agreed as the announcer reached the end of his count.

Farnsworth took a seat as a wave of bodies began to flood the hall. Diego grinned as he counted the images. He pointed to one of himself drawn as Conan and pointing his huge sword like some kind of lewd prop.

"I don't know anything about art, but I like that one."

Farnsworth rolled his eyes as Diego ribbed him.

"Do you see that there are *eight* that are clearly *you*?"

Farnsworth opened his mouth to speak, and then yanked his hood low and stiffened as if he'd just sat in Old Sparky. Diego looked at him sidelong when his partner kicked his foot and nodded over his shoulder.

Turning, Diego found a busty woman dressed in a white leotard. It was only two minutes into the convention and the chesty woman had already begun spilling out of her Powergirl costume. Despite a thick frame, she wore her figure with such confidence that she oozed seductive energy.

She giggled as she ogled the artwork. "Ohmygod. I feel like I *know* that guy." She bent halfway over the table for a better look and nearly fell out of the diamond shaped cut away at her costume's chest.

Diego gasped and Farnsworth coughed and stood to try and slip away.

She introduced herself, engaging Farnsworth directly, "My name's Jessica. I love your art! Tell me about it."

Diego leaned closer to her as Farnsworth started coughing and gesturing with his hands, making a drinking motion. "Sorry about my partner," he interjected as Farnsworth backed away. "He has too... um... poop?"

"That's a pretty sweet Lobo costume," she said as Farnsworth escaped.

"Fraggin Main Man Slim Jim," he said.

Jessica didn't really pay much attention. Instead, she read the signage banner and grinned. "Partners in art... and so much more, right?" She winked.

Diego stiffened. He didn't know how she knew and so he merely shrugged and played dumb.

"I'll take that one," she pointed to a print of Farnsworth reimagined as a purple-hued pegasus with lizard legs; he held a sword in one hand. Only the arms belonging to a figure out of the scene were visible and they held a dominatrix-style riding crop. "I love it!" she exclaimed, jiggling all over with glee.

She turned it back to Diego. "You have to autograph it, though."

With a sigh, he did his best to match Quast's illegible scribble in the lower left hand corner. Jessica shot him a peculiar look as she traced it with her eyes, but said nothing. She thanked him and then moved down the hall to look over other vendors' items.

# 36

Deadpool

"Hello readers. I bet your wondering, 'who's this amazingly handsome guy in the red suit? He's like a way better Santa Clause who sniffs your hair when you sit on his lap.' I want you to know that I do indeed have a present. It's smaller than a bread box and may or may not be currently wrapped in my boxers."

Diego and Farnsworth both stared slack-jawed at the Deadpool cosplayer as he narrated his own scene. A concerned parent nearby covered her eight-year-old's ears and tried to navigate as far away as possible.

*"Who are you talking too?"* an exasperated Diego spat.

"No—oh, it's too late," Farnsworth sighed. "I should have told you. Never engage someone dressed as Deadpool. It's just a basic convention rule I have. Not unless you want to wind up going down the rabbit hole."

Deadpool sashayed nearer with a giggle. "Hehe. You said hole." The costume clad figure swung his hip up onto the table. "Whose healing factor do you think is stronger? Lobo or DP?"

Diego furrowed his brow with confusion.

"Abort. Abort," muttered Farnsworth.

*"I'm DP,"* the invader explained. Without missing a beat he asked, "Can I touch your muscles? They look so real."

"No."

He touched them.

"Oooooh. You guys are *partners*. I'm thinking you guys must totally be into DP, then." He stared at them in a long unflinching silence. Finally, he whispered, "I'm winking under my mask."

Diego scowled and stood. Partly, he'd hoped to intimidate the obnoxious jokester into leaving, but also the costumed nut-job's antics had blocked his view of the *Knights of the Illuvian Age* display.

The cosplayer put both hands on his cheeks as if frightened. "Would you like to touch my chimichanga? His name is Phil."

"I just want to sew this idiot's mouth shut," Diego murmured.

Farnsworth snapped at him, "No! You must never say that out loud." His expression turned suddenly serious. "In this kind of crowd, you could be attacked for saying that. I know you didn't know any better but..."

Diego shushed him.

Deadpool put a finger to Farnsworth's lip and cooed like the detective was a baby.

"I see him. Sheen," Diego said.

"You guys are awesome," Deadpool said, leaning back over the table. "Let's be best friends."

Farnsworth dropped a pre-made "Back in Five minues" sign on the table. The undercover cosplayers both got up and left, completely forgetting their weapons.

"Guys. Guys?" Deadpool stared at them as they walked, finally losing them in the crowd. "Hey readers, who wants some free artwork? If you answered Deadpole, you would've guessed... well, close enough to steal some pervy artwork."

He got up and stared at the art. "Oh my! *He's a pegasus and I love him!* I'll name you Squishy." He crawled behind the table.

"And then Deadpool rolled up the print and casually walked away," he said with a narrator-like tone. Deadpool rolled up the print and then walked away, bumping into a human-sized, violet rabbit.

# 37

## Follow the Bright Rabbit

A person dressed in a bright purple rabbit costume walked through the crowd and gave a big thumbs up to a massive guy in a Lobo costume. He sure had committed to wear that much body paint below his leather vest. The big dude barely acknowledged him with his Czarnian grimace.

Barely a few moments later, Sir Hops Alot spotted the most beautiful artwork he'd ever seen. Deadpool was obviously robbing the vendor. The bunny-man shrugged; what could a person expect when half the attending con population viewed "thief" as a legitimate class/job.

The antihero finished rolling up the last print he wanted and bumped into him.

"Ohithere! I was just, uh…"

Sir Hops Alot scanned the displays of hanging pages. A kind of supernatural reverence struck him when he laid eyes on a certain piece. "The prophecy," he whispered.

"Are there any more of that one?" Sir Hops Alot pointed to the display graphic of Farnsworth as a BDSM pegasus.

"Just the one hanging there. Special pricing for the next five minutes," Deadpool exclaimed, "free."

Sir Hops Alot leaned over the table and snatched the last image from the clips that help it in place. "Perfect!"

They both looked down each side of the aisle, expecting that someone might come to stop them. Nobody did, although a voice called out.

"I think I might have what you both need."

An Egyptian book peddler leaned back on a chair in his booth. He put a bookmark in an old and pale, leather bound text labeled *De Vermis Mysteriis* and motioned to them

Deadpool did a double take half expecting that he would be gone at second glance. "But you weren't... how did you... where did... are those fruit roll-ups?"

The man tilted his fez with a nod and offered the cosplayer one. His booth's sign read *Arcane Antiquities & Rare Texts.*

Sir Hops Alot stepped forward hesitantly, like a rabbit near a hawk's eyrie. From behind the mesh panels of his bulky rabbit mask his eyes scanned the stacks of dusty materials; sheaves of parchments and filigreed baubles lay strewn across the table as if they hadn't been moved in a hundred years.

His eyes caught the sigil inlaid upon the cover of a black, leather tome. "I-is that what I think it is? Is it real?"

The peddler moved aside a stack of *The King in Yellow* playbills and picked it up. He unclasped the cover and opened it to the title page which bore the waxing and waning ink lines indicative of a fountain pen. "Necronomicon - by Abdul Alhazred."

Before Sir Hops Alot could turn a page, the dark skinned man snapped the book shut; the cover seemed to reclasp of its own accord. "When you have need of such a delightful read, be sure to come back and see me," the vendor grinned. *"You will know when the time is right."*

"H-how much?" Sir Hops Alot's voice warbled. He licked his lips and swallowed hard to try and wet his suddenly dry throat.

The mysterious man smiled. "For you my friend? No charge. I would love to simply *lend it* to you."

Sir Hops Alot reached for the book and the man pulled it away. "Ah, ah, ah. Not yet... I said *when the time is right.* You will know when."

"Hey," Deadpool interjected. "You got any more of these?" He wrinkled up the fruit roll-up wrappers.

"Just take the whole box," the vendor sighed and sent them on their way.

# 38

Con Man

The two detectives meandered through the lazy crowds. They turned aside to look at whatever was in a nearby booth whenever the ex-con turned their direction.

Henry Sheen looked haggard and on edge, as if he hadn't slept in days. Diego and Farnsworth exchanged knowing looks... if they were able to follow the breadcrumbs that led Sheen here, certainly Gage Houdek could do likewise. Especially since at least two of his targets would be under one roof... three if he caught Sheen here as well.

Farnsworth scanned the crowd nervously, not that he or anybody else outside of Bratva knew what Zmei looked like. He glanced past a cluster of cosplayers including John Wick, Agent 47, and Altaïr Ibn-La'Ahad; Farnsworth felt certain that a professional hit-man would seem obvious if he ever spotted him.

They closed in just as Sheen turned unexpectedly. The three of them locked gazes and the criminal fled like a startled gazelle, dodging around con-goers as he scrambled.

Giving chase, Diego plowed his way through a cluster of people. Mabel Pines and two hobbits flew through the air like bowling pins.

Farnsworth veered around a break in the aisle and tried to flank him. A small crowd split aside to make room for him. A convention volunteer pushing a hospitality cart stacked high with ramen noodles stood like a deer in headlights and Farnsworth plowed through and tumbled to his knees, scattering the entire cart-load of contents across the floor.

He scrambled back to his feet and darted forward, crunching noodles underfoot. Sheen caught sight of him and pushed a rack of custom printed t-shirts into his path.

The clumsy detective caught a foot on it and stumbled. His legs tangled on his robed costume and sent him careening through a huge display of Funko Pop! toys. The stack toppled and momentarily pinned him beneath the great pyramid of disproportionate action figures. He howled a Wilhelm scream as he thrashed beneath the mountain of boxes.

Diego rounded a corner and turned away as the criminal snatched up a sword from a prop weapons vendor. He ducked beneath the criminal's wild, untrained slash and rolled to his side. The detective grabbed a sword and whirled to face Sheen; he slashed for the man who'd murdered his partner.

Sheen blocked the blow with a panicked howl. Diego's foam sword hit the metal edge of his opponent and collapsed into two pieces.

"Fraggin bastich!" the cosplaying Main Man yelled, whirling back to grab an actual metal weapon. Diego spun back to attack, brandishing a pair of Wolverine claws, but Sheen had already sprinted away as soon as the opportunity arose.

Farnsworth scrambled and thrashed beneath the pile, but something had a hold of his cloak. He yanked it free and knocked over any part of the exhibit that remained intact. He emerged from the chaos with smeared makeup and complete dishevelment. Spotting his partner chasing Sheen from the exhibit hall, he wriggled amid the boxes until he was free and then joined the chase.

Out of breath, but not wanting to fail his partner, Farnsworth hurried through the lobby and charged towards the street level access. Taking an angle around the crowd he almost beat his partner to the escalator.

The moving stair was packed with badge wearing event-goers. Sheen was already halfway up, wide-eyed but standing straight in his place with his hands on the rail.

"Hands were we can see em… Ride protocol," the security at the top and bottom muttered as if it was some kind of holy mantra.

Diego and Farnsworth crammed into the mouth of the escalator that moved at a pace designed to frustrate a snail. The bulky detective began picking his way through the riders, trying to catch up to the criminal.

At the top and bottom red-faced security guards screamed at Diego to stop. "Rules violation! Rules violation!" they howled and pointed.

Farnsworth stood rooted to his metal step, yelling for his partner to stop and follow the con's insane escalator policy. "Rick! Rick, I forgot to tell you about the escalators! Stay still!"

It was too late. Diego had his prey in his sights. He had Henry Sheen locked into his vision. He'd almost caught up to him when Sheen stepped onto the floor of the street level.

Barely an arm's length out of reach, the criminal hurried away from the event center and sprinted towards the exit.

Diego stepped off the escalator and onto the tile floor where he was immediately gang tackled by six security members who saw escalator enforcement as their life's primary calling. The under-cover officer screamed and struggled as more officers burst out from a nearby room and helped drag Diego away.

Farnsworth arrived at the top where two men stood expectantly. They tried to intimidate him by tapping their long flashlights in their hands.

"Are you with him?" one asked in a cracking voice.

"Yeah. He didn't know the rules… first timers, right…"

They immediately began clubbing him with their flashlights. "You've got to come with us!" they howled.

"Fine—ow! I'm coming. Ouch!" he yelled as he cooperated and tried to follow his partner.

"Stop resisting! You're coming with us," they insisted like a bunch of Volgon enforcers as they maintained a hail of furious, limp-wristed blows about the head. "Resistance is futile!"

Both detectives seethed, but knew they had to play along. Even if Sheen got away, they had to remain on site if they were going to capture Houdek before he could kill Wil Wheaton.

# 39

The Confather Part I

Confiscating their badges, the guards led the way through the service tunnels that led to the lowest utility sections.

Farnsworth followed his partner towards a makeshift cage where the power mad security team stored their prisoners. Inside it, a man crawled around on all fours, naked except for a Gandalf hat and beard; he cackled, happy for guests to join him. Another one sat in the opposite corner injecting heroine.

The closest guard kicked the cage. Hissing, the strange Gandalf darted to the far corner and quaked with anticipation. The junkie foamed at the mouth but didn't otherwise react.

Diego wrinkled his nose as they locked the gate. The bearded inmate in the hat smelled like crap and gin as he crawled slowly towards his new comrades.

"Well, well, well," laughed Harding, the same guard who had hassled them earlier. He leaned up against the wall and took a deep drag off of his vaping device. Harding held in the lungful and then blew a stream of birthday cake flavored smoke towards the cell. "Welcome to Convention Jail."

"Am I dreaming? I must be dreaming, or maybe someone drugged me?" Diego muttered under his breath. "It's like some kind of coked out *Wizard of Oz* stuff, here."

The naked wizard man crawled towards the vape smoke, salivating. The junkie cringed as Harding spun his e-cig machine around his finger as if he were a gunslinger; "Even *I* think your habit is disgusting," he wheezed.

"Nobody cares about your opinions, Jeremy! Go back to shooting smack you filthy junkie."

"It's my insulin."

"Whatever floats your boat, man."

Weird Gandalf got too close to the door.

"What'd I say—get back, Jeffrey!" Harding screamed, kicking the cage.

Jeffrey barked and snarled like a dog and tried to bite the guard's foot as if he had rabies. The sentries began arguing about what sort of awful things they should do to their new prisoners.

Suddenly, the lights went out leaving only the illuminated hallway behind them to provide an eerie back-lighting.

With a reverent air the guards began to whisper, "The Master is coming. The Master!"

Long shadows stretched along the corridor until finally, a man in a black robe darkened the door. Only his chin remained visible as he walked slowly, authoritatively, into the room.

The guards all bent a knee. "The Master is here!" they gibbered.

"What have we found, my minions?" The voice spoke with power.

Farnsworth's ears picked up. He stared at the figure and squinted in the darkness.

"Unworthy rules breakers," Harding said.

"Unworthy... Unworthy!" the others parroted as they buzzed like awed chimps in the dark.

"Perhaps these two interlopers..."

"I know that voice!" Farnsworth exclaimed. "You—you're Alan Tudyk."

"Uh. No I'm not," Tudyk tried to change his voice by shifting it an octave. "You can't prove anythi—dang it you guys!" He flung his shroud back. "Jeffrey, get out of there! Every time I bring you to a con this kind of stuff happens." Tudyk glared at Harding. "You guys have to stop this. I told you not to let my cousin drink too much." He muttered to himself, "Every single time."

"But what about these guys?" Harding said. "We can't just let them go unpunished."

Tudyk turned and stood straight. "I'm sort of in charge of the seedy underbelly of all cons," he said in something that sounded like a Godfather voice. He extended a hand. "If you kiss my ring and accomplish a task for me, I will secure your release."

Diego raised both eyebrows. The entire mission had descended into anarchy and his dumbfounded feet had anchored to the floor.

Farnsworth, already kneeling, chastised his partner. "Psst! When the Confather offers you a boon, take it!"

"Um..." Diego shook himself out of the fugue and knelt. "Yeah. Whatever. What is this task?"

Tudyk smiled. "There is a certain piece of artwork I have my eye on. I want you to find it and bring it to me: a handsome man drawn as a powerful pegasus and getting a spanking from his special friend." He eyed Farnsworth. "He looks kinda like that guy, but majestic... less pasty and covered in Jeffry's urine."

"Wha—gross!" Farnsworth shoved the drunkard away and threw his soiled cloak to the floor in disgust.

"Do you know the one?"

Diego nodded.

"Good. Then you're free to go. As soon as you bring it to me I'll put a ribbon on each of your badges, giving you VIP status and immunity."

Diego looked to Farnsworth for an explanation. "You get extra special treatment and certain perks like free soda."

Tudyk grimaced. "Yeah, sorry about that. The event center's cooling systems recently failed—the kitchens are both down for maintenance and renovations."

Farnsworth shrugged.

"Plus, my loyal worshipers won't hassle you anymore." He tossed them back their badges. He shifted back to his Confather voice. "Find it and bring it to me. I must have this one—it fits perfectly with my collection."

Tudyk snapped his fingers as he turned to leave. "Come along, Jeffrey. I've got some pressing matters to take care of—I may need you to go under cover."

"Like a dutch oven?" Jeffrey asked.

The Confather sighed. "I'm surrounded by idiots… and no. Now get out of there and put on your fuzzy pants. I have a mission for you"

Harding unlocked the cage and the detectives hurried back towards their booth as quickly as possible.

Tudyk looked at them both. "I really do mean it. Bring me that picture. It's… very important."

# 40

Cold War

People had clustered around the booth to ogle Quast's experimental artwork. Farnsworth and Diego had to push their way through in order to get back to their seats.

A few people asked questions and handed over money for prints. Most, finally face to face with the creator of such weirdly erotic materials wandered away, knowing better than to show too much interested in this kind of vendor's wares and accidentally wind up on a mailing list.

Diego rifled through the stack of reproductions but couldn't find any more of the pegasus prints. He frowned, but shrugged and figured he'd pull down the display one. The big detective scratched his head and stared at the empty spot where it had earlier hung.

Farnsworth joined his partner, looking worried. "It's gone."

Diego nodded, but didn't seem to think much of it. He turned and sat at the table. "I hope the Confather wasn't serious about all that nonsense."

A dark cloud filled Farnsworth's gut, but he ignored it and sat, hoping Diego was right. The crowd had thinned noticeably now that the celebrities had begun the meet-and-greet sessions. Autograph lines formed on the far side of the room, just a little ways away from the Goblin Hole's booth.

Applause went up from the crowd as Wil Wheaton emerged from the rear hallway. He bowed with a wave and took his seat at a table. Both men and women respectfully clapped and saluted him like he'd just made a clinch put on the PGA Tour or Wii Golf.

Next emerged Michael Dorn, Wheaton's former co-star from Star Trek the Next Generation. The actor, renown for being on more Star Trek films than any others, didn't wear his Klingon makeup or costume, although he did carry and swing around a sharp, metal bat'leth, the double-ended alien scimitar weapon.

The crowds, already enraptured with the younger man's upcoming *Knights of the Illuvian Age* project largely ignored the venerable Dorn. Except for one short, morbidly obese fanboy in a pink Spock costume who raised both fists and screamed as if his roller coaster called life had just sped through one huge loop.

Both actors took their seats at neighboring tables and initially refused to look at each other.

"Tell me again why *we* need to be in costume if the celebrities don't need them?" Diego crossed his arms and groused below his breath.

Farnsworth smiled at his partner. The crowds were a pretty even mix of cosplayers and folks in regular clothes. "It'll help us keep our cover."

Diego rolled his eyes and turned back to the celebrities. He scanned their lines for any kind of suspicious persons, but most of the con-goers had a certain euphoric look plastered to their faces. None of them had the hard jawline and cold eyes the detective expected to see on the mysterious Gage Houdek.

The bubbly blonde super-heroine from earlier hopped in front of their table. "Hey! Some jerk brony stole my print during a crazy-serious Settlers of Catan game. Do you have any..."

Jessica's eyes locked on Farnsworth who turned to the side, trying to hide himself. Without his pee-soaked hood and cloak, there was no way for the detective to maintain his disguise.

"Well... look what the cat dragged in. Moses Farnsworth." She relished his uncomfortable cringing for a few seconds and then scanned the rainbow booth banner. "Well… I guess it's all making sense now."

"No!" Farnsworth jumped to his feet. "I'm not gay."

Diego interjected and agreed, "We're not together. Even if he *was* gay, he wouldn't be my type."

She stared down her nose at them, not really buying any of what they were selling. Jessica turned her eyes to the large number of suggestive prints in which Farnsworth was obviously the artist's muse. "Riiiight. Listen, guys. This is a safe space…"

Farnsworth interrupted her and leaned close enough that only the three of them could hear. "You know that I was a cop."

"I honestly don't know what to believe about you anymore."

"We're under cover!" he snapped at her loud enough that two passersby overheard.

Diego called out loud enough to try and keep up their disguise. "All the time—under the covers. Just… being gay. Gay as a jaybird."

Jessica stifled a laugh at the obvious discomfort from the macho detective. "Now *that guy* I believe." Her hostile posture switched back into her normally effervescent demeanor.

As soon as Farnsworth relaxed she asked, "So why are you undercover at a comic-con of all places?"

"We can't tell you," Diego gruffed. He shot Farnsworth a look of disappointment, "My *partner* shouldn't even have said as much as he did."

Jessica shot the big guy a mischievous grin and bit her lower lip playfully while wrapping a finger through her hair. "I'm awfully curious and I won't tell anyone. I always get what I want; it's almost like I have *special powers*." She arched her shoulders back so that her bust line stuck out.

Diego tried to respond, but found himself suddenly confused and unable to put his words together.

Farnsworth jabbed him in the ribs and nodded to the VIP area. Dorn had thrown a bottle of water at Wheaton who got up and stormed off angrily into the crowd.

"We've gotta keep eyes on you know who," he hissed.

Both detectives snatched their sidearms from under the table and tucked them into their pockets. They leapt out of the booth and pushed their way through the droves of people. Jessica shrugged and followed.

# 41

Crushing Wesley

Something buzzed in the back of Farnsworth's mind like the Force. A seed of dread took root in the pit of his gut and he manically scanned the crowd in the lobby.

Glance, pass. Glance, pass. Glance... doubletake at the hottie who's catsuit had unzipped far too much to remain appropriate... pass. Glance, pass. One more look at the Catwoman.

Farnsworth rattled his head to clear the distractions. Up ahead, Diego plowed a furrow through the congregation. His partner looked back, keeping in contact nonverbally.

Diego pressed towards the rear of the area and Farnsworth crawled up a stairway that led to the upper level hallway which was marked prohibited. From the elevation he saw a circle of ninjas playing Ninja, some nekomimi girls licking their own arms and a bunch of pervs watching them through their cell phone cameras, a shoving match ensued between an Optimus Prime and Voltron over the use of an electrical outlet, and an impromptu dance party with the bridge crew from Star Trek TNG had a dance off. A Borg danced off against Data. Both performed the robot.

Diego looked up at his partner for directions. Farnsworth pointed the way—he was sure he'd just seen Wheaton rushing towards the corner furthest from the doors.

Security guards spotted Farnsworth and began shoving their way through the throng in order to get at him. With Diego headed in the right direction, the shorter detective glanced around nervously, sure that the Confather wouldn't show leniency a second time.

He took one hesitant step higher as the guards formed a mob at the base of the stairs. They tapped their flashlights against their palms like billy clubs and gave him a menacing smile.

Luckily, Farnsworth didn't recognize any of them from their earlier incarceration. He looked at the cordoned off platform above him. It looked like the only way was up.

Across the lobby someone shouted a string of profanities and animal sounds. The lynch mob that had trapped Farnsworth turned as one to face the staircase on the opposite side. The Deadpool cosplayer danced on the landing half a flight up.

"Yoo-hoo! Hey Paul Blart—come and get me!"

He dropped the skin-tight, red trousers and exposed his naked bottom. Mooning the crowd below. He jiggled up and down like he was twerking and went full testicle.

A child screamed in terror. The security team turned as a single unit and charged for the opposite stairwell, leaving only one pimply officer to try nabbing Farnsworth.

Deadpool pulled up his pants and saluted Farnsworth who returned the gesture. Just as security closed in, the psychotic cosplayer leapt from his perch, grabbed some vinyl signage, and swung to the floor where he tucked and rolled through a trio of pleather-clad, gender-bending catwomen and a zombie Jesus, splitting the seven and ten. He jumped to his feet and pushed over the two nuns each holding a cat-persons' leash and dabbed. "That's a spare! Twelve points!"

The obnoxious cosplayer fled into the crowd, losing himself in a cadre of Deadpoolified costumers congaing as a mini-parade. Someone's Dogpool in a service animal harness humped a Care Bear amidst all of the chaos.

Farnsworth checked his partner's position one final time and then hopped up onto the landing as the inept guard stumbled up the steps and after him. Swinging his legs over the guard rail, Farnsworth shimmied his way down to the support pillar and slid ten feet to the ground.

He shoved his way through the oblivious throng until he heard the music from the Star Trek dance party. An earsplitting noise came from the boom-box's speakers. Those close enough to the federation's gyrations realized it wasn't just hipster Picard's terrible mix-tape; a woman screamed and the detective thought he knew the voice.

Farnsworth busted his way through the wall of bodies even as the sci-fi dancers fled the circle they'd carved out from the crowd. He found Jessica on her knees with blood splattered across her face. Diego stood next to her, staring in shock at the body leaking blood upon the floor. A bloody butterfly knife lay near the corpse.

"Houdek," Farnsworth spat as he stared at the body.

Wil Wheaton was dead.

# 42

The Mirror Universe

"It's not him," Farnsworth said as he turned over the bearded Wesley Crusher. "It's just some dude dressed up like Wheaton from the old television series."

At the edges of the slowly collapsing dance circle, a few people clapped. Others cheered or took selfies with the body in the background. The crowd clearly thought this was some kind of clever act.

Jessica was beside herself. "I saw him." She trembled, but took comfort as she leaned into Diego's arms. "Long dark hair, suit coat. Dressed like a normal." She pointed to a door that Diego guessed led into a service hallway.

Farnsworth crouched by the body. "Go get him," he nodded. "I've got this." He gestured to Diego. "But give me your vest."

Still dressed mostly as Lobo, he shrugged off the garb. Diego charged towards the corridor's entry, now bare chested.

Farnsworth wrapped as much of the body under the vest and his own shirt to keep from leaving a blood trail to the nearby janitor's closet. In case they didn't catch Zmei, they would need to reset the trap and try again—and any kind of panic shutting down the convention wouldn't help.

He looked up and watched Jessica chase Diego through the door. Farnsworth hoped she would help rather than make the situation worse.

Jamming the body in the closet, he pulled out the mop as he thumbed his cell phone. He'd have to send Quast a message and get someone discreet down to take care of the body after TrollCON closed for the evening and shifted to the various hotel parties.

Farnsworth watched the hydraulic assist on the hall door slowly close, separating him from Diego.

Diego charged ahead, methodically checking the angles to clear the path from any danger. He turned towards the footsteps behind him and nearly drew his gun on Jessica.

Before he could demand that she leave, Jessica insisted, "I can help you. I saw the killer."

The service hallway branched off with short corridors that terminated in banquet halls and meeting rooms. Stacks of chairs, loading dollys, and service carts lined the halls where employees had left them lie. It appeared like some kind of a maintenance maze.

Both of them wrinkled their noses as they rounded a corner. "Refrigerant," Jessica pointed to the greenish liquid puddled by the base trim.

Diego kept moving, not really caring why she could identify so specific of a liquid.

In the distance, around at least one corner, a latch echoed loudly as a door clicked shut.

"I know where he went!" Jessica exclaimed. "There's another lobby on the other side of the convention center—it's the sixth street entrance."

Diego nodded and sprinted forward to try and close the distance. Winded by the jog, Jessica tried to catch up.

The hallway suddenly erupted in pandemonium. Costumed denizens of the halls jumped out to bar his passage. Their brightly colored fabrics and masks whirled like a kaleidoscope.

Jumping atop a chair a scrawny man dressed as a Pink Panther, except that he wore a leather thong, screamed, "Another intruder! The Bronies continue to violate the sacred truce and cross through the neutral zone!"

Diego barely slowed as he looked back at Jessica, she pushed and shoved at the costumers who clawed at her. "Furries! Run!"

The detective plowed through as the furries raised fists high, brandishing makeshift weapons and costume props like some kind of My Little Pony Mad Max hybrid.

Pink Panther yelled, "We must defend our honor and our borders!"

His minions screamed their support. "Justice for Jonah!"

Jonah, a turquoise leopard, leaned against a cement block wall with his mask off. He nursed a bloody nose—probably from Houdek—and mumbled, "I'm okay, you guys. Really."

The cry for blood only intensified as Jessica caught up to Diego. Together, they burst through the line and fled with thirty angry furries chasing them like a faux-fur flood.

Directly ahead, a bare-chested, overweight man in a mullet and neon spandex crawled atop a stack of tables and howled. "The furries want to go to war with the Bronies? So be it; Bronies Assemble!"

The other side of the hallway suddenly filled with humanoid men and a few women wearing fake ears and brightly colored hair, tails, and wigs. Someone screamed from their rear, "Super magic friendship beat-down!"

Diego grabbed Jessica's hand and led her through the oncoming horde. He lowered his shoulder and pushed through with relative ease. Bronies bounced off his tough exterior with whimpers and squeaks.

"Oh no!" Jessica said beneath her breath. "It's a full-blown turf war beneath the Furries and the Bronies... the prophecy is finally coming true."

Just as they emerged from the crowd of colorful, fluffy anarchy, the two forces collided. They wheezed and shrieked as they smashed against each other. "You were supposed to be one of us!" a furry screamed. "For Equestria!" several Bronies shouted as they curb-stomped a fox-girl. "We're twenty percent cooler than you!"

Diego and Jessica finally crashed through the fire door and into the sixth street lobby. Immediately they spotted a long-haired man stepping into a group of non-Japanese Japanese schoolgirls. With his broad shoulders and dark suit he stuck out like a sore thumb, no matter how he tried to hide.

"There!" Jessica pointed.

Diego sprinted ahead and speared him from the back, tackling him like an eager linebacker. The man screamed with a feminine shriek as the detective took him down.

Pinning him to the ground, a brown wig fell from the costumed genderbender. She howled for help and the cosplaying schoolgirls rained down fists and feet upon detective Diego. They screamed their mantra. "Cosplay is not consent! Cosplay is not consent!" One woman began blowing her rape whistle like she was selected for a solo at a concert.

Barely able to see through the flurry of fists and gang-style beat-down the anime group delivered, he relinquished his grip on the suspect and scrambled to safety.

Jessica shrugged. "Sorry," she said. "It looked like him at first."

Diego frowned but didn't say anything. He walked in silence and took the long way around to find his partner, perking up as the announcer stated on the loudspeaker that Wil Wheaton had returned to the autograph signing tables after taking a short break.

He checked his watch. With almost one day down out of several, he knew this would prove to be a *very* long weekend.

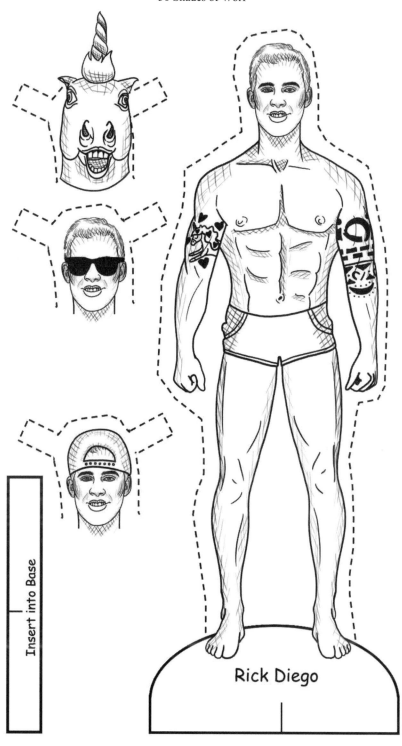

Insert into Base

Rick Diego

Post pics of your weirdest scenes to
#50ShadesofWorf

Post pics of your weirdest scenes to
#50ShadesofWorf

# PART FIVE

## DAY 2

# 43

Day 2

Rick Diego rested his head against the cold brick and leaned against the urinal as he closed his eyes. The day had barely begun and he didn't know why, but he felt hung over; the mental exhaustion had caught up.

He tightened his nostrils and tried not to inhale too deeply. The toilets had begun to smell as expected, but pockets of the general population had also begun to emit a mysterious aura that no amount of Axe body spray could mask—something like a post-asparagus musk.

Wrinkling his nose in disgust, Diego washed his hands and read the sign posted on the mirror. *Achievement unlocked: Hands washed.* He guessed he might've been one of the proud few to earn such a prestigious award.

The detective splashed a little water on his face and began strapping on the layers of leather that made up his Judge Dredd costume. He begun to wonder exactly why his partner owned as much leather as he did when Jack Sparrow sauntered through the lavatory.

Odors didn't lie, and he most certainly wasn't faking the rum-drunk walk as he staggered to the urinal. "Release the Krakken!" the pirate yelled as he unzipped his pants and pissed all over the wall, fully two inches left of the privy.

Diego sighed, put on his helmet, venturing back towards the craziness that was TrollCON. He got close to his table and spotted Farnsworth trying his best to shoo away a booth barnacle who wouldn't stop talking.

The balding man with an itchy neckbeard stood barely four foot ten, probably weighed around three-hundred pounds, and smelled like he'd eaten *all the asparagus.* Diego wasn't certain he was speaking English, even.

"...that's why Motoko Kusanagi is totally my waifu," he said in a grating, high-pitched voice. He glanced down the aisle at a teenage girl wearing the character's skin-tight bodysuit and licked his chapped lips. "I think she could learn to love me," he said in a border-line whisper.

Diego stopped right in front of the booth and stood uncomfortably close to the diminutive troll. He stared him down.

El creepo cringed and took a step back. Nothing about Diego's demeanor indicated he wanted to take the man up on the *Free Hugs* offer advertised by his pit-stained t-shirt.

"I see you looking at my daughter," he lied. The detective waved to the anime cosplayer as if he knew her. She waved back without explanation.

"Oh, um. There's Bulma way over there. Maybe she's looking for some dragonballs." The human-hutt hybrid waddled away as quickly as his kowakian monkey-lizard legs could carry him.

"Whew!" exclaimed Farnsworth. He reached under the table and pulled out an aerosol can. He hoped the febreeze was capable of defeating the lingering cloud in mortal kombat.

Diego plopped down into his chair so they could continue watching for their targets. Wheaton wouldn't be back at the table for a while, and Dorn seemed all the better for it.

"Is it just me, or did the craziness actually amplify overnight?" he asked as he removed his sweaty helmet. An unmistakable weariness colored his voice.

Farnsworth nodded and jotted notes down on their subjects. Kubrick had announced a huge panel to discuss *Knights of the Illuvian Age* with Wheaton on the following day. He was making a killing selling t-shirts and last minute additions to the

Kickfunder. Only those participants in shirts or who gave online got admission to the exclusive panel and discussion.

Diego watched his weird, spandex-clad partner. He could tell Farnsworth wanted to join that panel in the worst possible way, but refused to let his current duties slide.

"What's the big deal with this Illuvian Knights book, anyway?"

Farnsworth brightened. "I can hardly believe you haven't heard of it. Groundbreaking, exhilarating," he realized he was talking like a newspaper review. "It builds a very real, very big world where some unknown heroes, the little guys, rise up and make it a better place. Elves, dwarves, all of those kinds of fantasy elements that sort of make the world somehow better — certainly different."

He got quiet for a moment. "Not everybody is good at life. For people who don't feel like they fit in," he motioned to the crowd around them, "fantasy helps them escape those bad feelings. We're not stuck on the outside anymore. We're finally important... and I honestly believe that *everyone* feels like that at some point in their life."

Diego listened with thin lips. He nodded measuredly, barely perceptible.

Farnsworth pulled a book out of his duffel. He handed the worn and dogeared copy of *Knights of the Illuvian Age* to his partner who opened the cover flap and spotted a scribbled signature.

"I got this signed by Sharyn J.R.R.K. McCrumb two years ago... just before she died." He put it in Diego's hands. "Take it."

Diego could only stare at the book. He wasn't quite sure how to respond. Before he could even muster a "Thank You" a group of security officers marched down the aisle like stormtroopers led by the smug officer Harding.

They stopped at the detectives' booth and Harding dropped a note in front of them. It had been folded up into a triangular paper-football shape.

"The Confather thought it prudent to send you a message. Also, you guys keep leaving your booth unattended. You can't do that... Con policy. Next time, you might come back and there will be nothing left," Harding grinned.

Threat delivered, he turned a 180 on his heels with military-like precision. One of his escorts didn't understand the move and Harding stepped right into him. Both men fell to the ground and Harding hurled insults at him that he'd ripped off from any number of old cartoons. "Get off of me you imbecilic buffoon!" He crawled to his feet, muttered, "Out of my way, you lamebrain dunderhead," and then stormed off.

The two detectives looked at each other. "I guess Tudyk really likes his erotic horse art."

# 44

Stretching Legs

Farnsworth unfolded the note that had been sent by the vengeful Tudyk and read. "Give me the print by the end of the day or there will be CONsequences." A crudely drawn horse head that dripped blood was drawn on the bottom half of the page.

"Didn't you get any more printed after yesterday?"

Diego shrugged. "Sorry. I guess it slipped my mind. I'll get to it today at some point."

Farnsworth crossed his arms. "I hope so—it'll be difficult to stay on-mission if con security is after us... at the very least, I wouldn't doubt if they shut down our stand."

Diego didn't have any particular inclination to wander the panels or vendor halls, but after Harding's threat he didn't want to remain stuck at the table a moment longer.

In the distance, a few convention employees came out and began staging Wheaton's table for the autograph and photo sessions that would begin soon. Dorn merely glared at them.

A voluptuous, blond Sailor Moon broke their line of visibility. Jessica ambled towards their booth and leaned up against it. "Nice Chunk costume," she identified Farnsworth by his Voltron paladin outfit.

Both detectives turned to look at her.

She raised her hands defensively. "Okay, I know I messed up yesterday, but I want to help," she tried to make her case.

"Done," Diego said, quickly rising to his feet. "You can watch our booth so we can get a closer look at the..." he floundered and pointed. "At that stuff."

The big guy maneuvered around the table, barely squeezing past the busty anime girl, and escaped with Farnsworth in tow.

"Just keep an eye on everything for us," Farnsworth said.

Jessica plopped down at the table, not quite expecting the hand she'd been dealt. "Wait! How much do you sell the prints for?"

"Don't care," Diego hollered back at the pouting cosplayer.

She growled only momentarily as she leaned forward over the table. The drooping neckline of her costume quickly attracted a small crowd of male customers who suddenly found themselves very interested in Quast's artwork.

Diego and his partner worked the crowd and looked for the best angles to continue their surveillance. They skirted the edge of Kubrick's displays, careful not to linger too close.

Tensing as they drew near to someone, Diego locked eyes on a man in a well-fit suit. He spoke some phrases in Russian as they got closer. He reached slowly towards his weapon as Farnsworth put a hand on his arm and shook his head *no*.

"He's in costume," the detective whispered. "You know John Wick, right?"

Diego shook his head.

"You'd like him. I imagine he's basically *your* back-story before you joined the police force." Farnsworth led them further away from the assassin costumer in a suit and further towards their targets.

"How many different assassins and hit-men can these people dress up as?" he whispered back.

The detectives casually weaved through the crowds, drawing ever closer to the velvet roped VIP area. Farnsworth nudged Judge Dredd and pointed.

Wheaton stepped from behind the curtains that hemmed in the area from a makeshift greenroom in the back. He'd opted to dress in a Klingon costume with rather poorly applied makeup—though it helped him remain identifiable despite the costume.

Those lining up for autograph sessions cheered, although Michael Dorn, who'd made a living off of portraying the Klingon, Worf, glared daggers at him. Dorn stiffened and stood, exiting through the curtains to take advantage of the green room.

"You don't think he'll be a problem, do you?" Diego asked.

"What? No. I'm sure it's just a little fight between friends."

Diego nodded, but decided to stick around. A few moments later he spotted a weasely and unshaven camera man meandering through the velvet ropes. He turned his ball cap backwards and stuck out his tongue as he grabbed shots of women's feet. He took his art seriously—even if he violated protocol by neglecting to ask for permission.

A trio of Sailor Moon cosplayers cringed. They turned around and shifted in line as they tried to get away from his lens.

Diego shook his head as he crushed the decorative rope in his fists. This wasn't something he could help with unless he risked breaking cover.

Suddenly, the curtains parted and the crowd gasped. Creepy photo-boy turned and began snapping photos with his convention employee badge flapping behind him.

Dorn flung the veil wide and leapt towards Wheaton. High above his head he brandished a shiny, metal weapon. Diego couldn't identify the sword-like thing, but the actor obviously meant to kill him. Wheaton recoiled—the look of terror frozen on his face.

In a flash, he had his weapon in his hand and his sights trained on Michael Dorn.

The camera clicked over and over, capturing every microsecond.

Farnsworth grabbed his partner's arm and lowered the gun before Diego knew what had happened. Dorn and Wheaton froze in place. Moments later the crowd began to cheer; cell phones came out and captured the staged scene.

"It's a photo-op," Farnsworth insisted.

The actors finally gave up the pose as an announcement came from the convention center's loudspeakers informing attendees how they could win a real Klingon bat'leth by registering at an autograph table with either of the Star Trek alums. "Winner must be present at the Knights of the Illuvian Age panel tomorrow!"

Diego finally relaxed and holstered his very-real firearm. "Sorry. Something about this whole thing has got me high strung."

Luckily Farnsworth's costume choice for the detective allayed any suspicion. "I think the cafeteria has decaf... they brought it in from street vendors since the kitchens are still down."

Diego nodded. "You may be right. Stay here and keep an eye on things. I'm going to go check out that meeting room where they're doing that panel tomorrow."

# 45

The Confather Part II

Alan Tudyk seethed with anger from underneath the throne he'd had assembled out of a bucket and empty cases of Mountain Dew. He glared at his officer from beneath a fully licensed Star Wars Emperor Palpatine cloak.

"You're telling me that you have no way of identifying the man who embarrassed a whole team of my guards?"

The guard cowed beneath his voice. "N—no, sir. But we did get this photo." He held up a grainy print from a security camera. Deadpool mooned the crowd with full back door nudity.

"I can't identify a man by his testicles!" Tudyk shrieked. "I mean, maybe Harding can... the guy does vape, after all." He shook away the notion.

"What do you think we're going to do—ask every Deadpool cosplayer to drop trow and show us their dingleberries?"

One of his security guards looked very eager at the notion.

"We can't do that!" He exclaimed, quietly adding, "not again. We can't afford another mishap like last time." He paused. "The least we can do is be discreet about it."

Harding suddenly burst into the clandestine throne-room located deep in the underbelly of the convention. He brandished his radio. "I've just gotten a report, sir!"

Tudyk motioned for him to continue.

Fear glinted in Harding's eyes. "It may very well be the end of days." His voice warbled. "There has been a fight... in the back hallways. It's the furries and the bronies again."

The Confather stiffened. "The prophecy."

Harding nodded. "This can only end in tragedy."

"Gentlemen, if we cannot bring order to the galaxy, these idiots will destroy it. Do you have any idea the impact an all-out war between the furries and the bronies will have? It could very well destroy the con scene as we know it. Do *you* guys want to go back to working at mall pretzel shops after a taste of power?"

A chorus of negatives rippled through the nearby guards.

Tudyk snapped his fingers. "Then somebody get me surveillance on the rival factions." He shouted an order to clarify, "And relevant footage only! I don't need six hours of random fursuits behaving inappropriately or another bronies gone wild video."

The soldiers nodded and departed.

Tudyk yelled after them. "Like, don't throw it away if you have any of those videos. Label it and set it aside like normal. I'll watch it later."

Hopefully Jeffrey could be of some future assistance on the matter. Sometimes a single pawn could win an entire game of checkers... Tudyk didn't know how to play chess, but he knew what a choking hazard was and how to hide game pieces inside the snack bowl. Game night was serious business at his house.

The Confather slumped into his throne under the weight of such leadership. Its cardboard pieces collapsed and he tipped off his bucket. "Ah crap."

# 46

Danny

Quast walked down the alley and met a haggard man dressed in a second-hand coat. "Are you Danny D?"

He nodded and leaned against the wall behind a dumpster. "You ain't from around here, are you?"

She shook her head.

"What you looking for, honey?"

"I was told you might be able to score me some Big H?"

Danny eyed her up and down, looking for track marks. He didn't see any, but finally he shrugged. "You got cash?"

Quast nodded.

The dealer grinned. "And what's to stop me from just takin it from you?"

"The two plain clothes police officers on either end of the alley." The four officers rushed towards them with guns drawn.

Danny grabbed her by the wrist and pulled a gun and put it to her head. "Everybody calm down or this little lady gets it!"

The officers slowed.

Quast scowled and pushed the gun away. He tried to grapple her into a tight hold but she head-butted him and then kneed him in the groin.

"I had three brothers," she explained to her fellow officers. "I was never in any real danger."

The smaller woman stood over him. "Danny Di Santo. You're under arrest."

He sneered through his bloody mouth. "You got nothing on me," he laughed. "I didn't even have any drugs. This is entrapment... police brutality," he began to howl

"You had a gun. As a felon that's against the law."

Di Santo cackled. "A fella can't own a squirt gun no more, either?"

Quast kicked the gun. It rattled on the asphalt with a hollow, plastic sound.

"That's okay," Quast droned in her monotone. "I know a lot about you, Mr. Di Santo. Really, I just wanted some info. But if you don't want to cooperate I'll settle for detaining you for twenty four hours while we pass on the word that you helped your old cellmate rip off the Bratva for hundreds of millions of dollars' worth of coke."

Di Santo's face fell. "Wait. No, it didn't go down like that."

"I'm sure the Brotherhood will be very understanding." She tried to roust him.

The ex-con went limp and tried to negotiate from the ground. "Wait, wait, wait. I'm sure I can find some kind of way to help you... but *discretely*."

"I know about your history with Henry Sheen, that you did time together and that you somehow got hooked in with a low level gig for Bratva because Sheen vouched for you... and I know you're still working for them." She fixed him with a stern glare.

Di Santo nodded, silently acknowledging her information.

"I just have a few gaps in my knowledge. You are going to tell me more..."

# 47

Casing the Con

Rick Diego strolled through the lobby, navigated the hallways, and eventually found the room where tomorrow's *Knights of the Illuvian Age* panel would be held. He ducked his head in and whistled.

The massive room had barely been filled for its current panel. He meandered through the rear of the enormous facility, exercising as much discretion as possible.

He could barely see the front of the room where a stage had been set up. As he got closer he found a panel of middle-aged white men in sweatpants arguing over who the best Batman was on the small and big screen. Passions flared; spittle flew; neck-beards were scratched. It was perhaps more violent than the final moments of a typical, family Monopoly game.

Diego stiffened and chose not to pay attention to such a seemingly trivial thing that might bring friends to blows... although he would certainly enjoy seeing *that*.

Calculating that there were over a thousand seats in the room, he noted the number and placement of the exits. Some opened back into the hallways which emptied into the lobby, and others spilled into the parking lots of the convention center.

A heavy set of curtains concealed everything behind the stage. Diego sneaked as close to the drapery as possible and then checked the room. The thirty or so people in the audience were so engrossed in the debate that he could have been dragging bells behind him and still been practically invisible.

Diego slipped beyond the curtains and found a rear entrance, as he suspected. He opened the door and stuck his head in. The smells of heavy musk and synthetic fur rolled over him.

"Furries," he growled, identifying the network of service halls he'd seen before. Diego took a black marker he kept in his pocket and scribbled three quick stars on the lower corner of the door in case he'd need to find his way here in the future.

The detective's phone buzzed and he checked the caller ID. Jennifer Quast—even *she* might seem like a breath of fresh air from the absurdity that surrounded the convention center. Diego coughed and sniffled, trying to override the pungent odor of furry.

*Fresh air. Ha.*

He answered it. "It's Diego. Give me some good news."

# 48

Uprising

Pink Panther stood on a stack of chairs in the lair they'd carved out of the network of halls in the back alleys. They'd barricaded themselves in a remote area and formed walls made out of spare tables tipped up on their ends.

"Brothers and sisters," he called out, "the Bronies have launched another salvo in this war that has been brewing for quite some time. Petey the Parrot and Vixen Gentleplumes were attending a panel on Politics as represented by Weird Al Yankovic lyrics when a group of Bronies forcibly removed their headpieces and exposed them to the public."

A gasp rippled through the crowd. Moments later a low growl replaced it. Murmurs whispered the thing they all knew was coming. "War."

Pink Panther, a long-time fixture on the convention circuit stoked the fires of conflict. "Long have we been patient with our younger cousins, but they seem to have issued a call to battle and the furries must answer!"

A chorus of howls and yips rose up.

"Is anyone here a good strategist... maybe you're pretty decent at Risk or Settlers of Catan or something? Cheaters are welcome, so anyone with a wealth of Uno experience is encouraged to respond."

The fursuits mostly cocked their heads and looked one to another. In the middle of the pack, a single purple paw raised.

"Sir Hops Alot?"

He took several small bounds forward until he stood at the front with the leader. "I know of a way. It may seem like a nuclear option, but my gut tells me its right... perhaps we should utilize the arcane arts to finish this once and for all?"

Sir Hops Alot handed him the artwork he'd swiped alongside Deadpool one day earlier. "There is a vendor here. I do not think he is everything that he seems. Right after I found this, I found *him*."

Pink Panther leaned forward. "Tell me more."

# 49

Breakthrough

"What have you got for me, Quast?" Diego asked.

She explained how she'd apprehended Danny Di Santo earlier in the day and been able to pry some information from him.

"Sheen got Di Santo a job working entry level stuff for Bratva when he left prison. After Sheen took the fall for the crime, he embarrassed the prosecutors while on the stand by reneging on his end of the bargain; that made him pretty much untouchable in prison. Bratva even let him keep the cash. Sheen was supposed to turn it over to the cops as part of the witness protection deal for him and his family, but Sheen refused. It was apparently a deal breaker for him."

"Wait a second," Diego spluttered. "Did you say Sheen had family? I didn't see any record, and I checked for it."

"Yes. He had a mother and father that went into witness protection. They died of health complications two years before Sheen's release."

"His family *still got protection after he killed the deal?*"

"Yes," Quast confirmed. "They were already in the wind by the time Sheen backed out of the deal."

Diego paused in thought, that wasn't normal practice—but he remembered that the prosecution had been so flustered that they simply cut bait and ran on the case; Sheen had singlehandedly sunk it by flipping on them. "What else do you have. Anything on the weird comic book angle at McCloud's murder?"

"Bratva kept all the details about the cocaine's distribution separate from other loose ends in order to prevent this exact kind of thing from happening. Sheen got Di Santo a low-level job on the street, but he was able to stumble onto enough details that he and his buddy could set up the hit on the drug operation... Di Santo also said there was no love lost between Sheen and McCloud. He hated him—talked about him all through prison."

"Enough to build such an elaborate trap?"

"Possibly," Quast acknowledged.

Diego paused and tapped his lip. "But he never mentioned comic books?"

"Di Santo never saw Sheen read anything, let alone comic books. Although, he did say that Sheen renewed a couple comic book subscriptions while incarcerated, but those magazines never arrived at the prison."

"I'm thinking there's still more to this story," Diego said. "Keep digging." He ended the call.

# 50

The Kevin Smith Non-Cameo

Farnsworth sat at the table next to Jessica. An odd, electrical tension sizzled in the air around them—odd even for TrollCON.

Diego returned, hanging up his cell phone after getting the updated info from Quast. He took his seat and noticed his presence seemed to neutralize some of the intense energy between his booth-mates.

Boba Fett, in full Mandalorian armor, approached the table. A second Mandalorian approached from the other side, blocking the path of the first.

Number One cocked it's helmeted head. "Are you one of the guys from the cosplay meetup group?" Fett's feminine voice asked.

Number two didn't respond, true to the Boba Fett character.

"Joe?" she asked. "Bob? Frank? Steve?" Finally, she ran out of options.

She reached out and took off Fett's helmet. The actor wore a rubber horse mask beneath it. She took off the horse mask to reveal Deadpool.

Busting a gut, the female Mandalorian moved on.

Deadpool turned to the artist table. "Hey guys! Didja miss me?"

"Meh," Jessica and Farnsworth toyed with the overly serious cosplayer. Diego flat out said, "No... who are you again?"

Deadpool faked heartbreak. "Don't tell security. Apparently they're looking for me—I had to come in disguise. I was going to come as a cognito, but didn't know what that was."

Jessica eyed him up and down. This particular Deadpool cosplayer took his gig pretty seriously. "You sure like to go deep into character, huh?"

"Soooo deep. We're talking inches. *Plural.*" He giggled and held up two fingers. "Here's a fun fact," he shifted gears like trucker on a go-kart. "My furry buddy Wolverine can't be Jewish."

Diego raised an eyebrow while the other two smirked. "I don't get it."

"I'd give you a demonstration," he said, "but I didn't see any corndogs at the concessions area to use as a prop."

"I heard that the kitchens are down for repairs," Jessica explained. "Everything had to be brought in from outside vendors this year. Kinda limits the options."

"Oh my glob!" Deadpool slapped his cheeks and started dancing up and down like Kevin McCallister with a full bladder. He pointed "Tyrion Lannister is a Blackhawks fan!"

A bearded little person turned his face to barely glare at the offensive remarks which he'd clearly heard. His hockey jersey hung to his knees and he tried to ignore the comments, though his quickened pace was a giveaway that he'd heard the quip.

Deadpool wouldn't let his new friend escape so easily. "Ohmygod, ohmygod, ohmygod!" he fan-girled. "I know who you are! You're chibi Kevin Smith?"

He set his jaw and glared daggers at the anti-hero cosplayer. His voice was firm. "My name is Mark, thank you, and I'm just here to meet Dan Jurgens and get my Superman 75 autographed. Now leave me alone, please."

"You must be a South Pole elf." Deadpool put his hands on his hips and crouched as if he addressed a child.

Mark stared down—stared up—at the cosplayer. "Do not..."

"Wait. Does Santa know you're out of the workshop?"

Mark screamed with frustration.

"Oh cute—now you're baby Groot... yay!."

The tiny hockey player slugged him right in the beans. "Heal from that, jackass!" Mark started kicking Deadpool while he was down, clutching his nards and groaning through the demented laughter. A security guard rushed over and tackled the little person, wrestling the diminutive, feral man to the ground.

The guard yanked off Mark's visitor badge and then dragged the belligerent, cursing dwarf by his shirt. "Hey," the pizza faced security guard recognized Deadpool by his mask. "I'm gonna have to ask you to show me your testicles for, uh, research purposes."

Deadpool began peeling off the Mandalorian armor. "I'll be right here when you get back" He gave a thumbs up and stepped out of the craft-foam girdle.

As soon as the guard disappeared Deadpool began exiting. "I don't think that boy's old enough to buy me the prerequisite drink. It's like Mama-pool used to say, 'never give away for free what the boys are willing to pay for.'"

The red-clad costumer disappeared into the crowd.

A few moments of silence passed, swallowed up by the awkward silence that ensued. "Why did that all seem par for the course?" Diego asked.

Another lull followed and the angst rolling off of Jessica seemed to intensify.

"So are we just going to not talk about it?" she finally asked, breaking the silence that Diego had so thoroughly appreciated.

Farnsworth sat straight, like he'd been shocked with a cattle prod. He tried to dodge the conversation. "I'm not entirely sure I know what you're talking about."

She fixed him with a glare and raised an eyebrow. "I'm talking about last year at this very same convention. You stood me up and left me stranded in the hotel all by myself! Not a very gentlemanly thing to do."

Farnsworth turned a shade of red normally reserved for bears, beets, and Battlestar Galactica.

"I mean, I get it if you didn't want to come up to my hotel room, but you could have just said as much rather than ghosting me and then avoiding me for an entire year. And for the record, you certainly seemed to have been flirting with me pretty hard up to that point."

Fumbling over his words, Farnsworth stammered. "Sorry... I was embarrassed. I got lost in the lobby and my phone died so I couldn't contact you." He stared at his feet. "Dropping out of the con circuit just seemed easier than the alternative."

Diego leaned back, stiff as a board, trying to stay out of the conversation, but Jessica would have none of it. She leaned into the larger detective. "You would never do that to a girl like me, would you?"

"Um..."

"Maybe you could learn something from your partner, Farnsy," she pouted. "Besides, I've moved on. I just wanted some closure." Jessica crossed her arms over her ample bosom.

"Well so have I." Farnsworth turned away slightly.

Diego's phone chirped.

"Speaking of Quast..." Diego reached for his mobile when Jessica stood up, grabbed the bigger detective by the face, and kissed him full on the lips.

In utter shock, Diego remained completely stiff, unsure how to respond. He still held the ringing phone in his hand, remaining as still as a statue.

Jessica pulled away, and then licked his face once. Finally done with Diego, Jessica gave a *hmph* like chuff to Farnsworth and walked away.

Diego could only shake his head and mutter something about how complicated this case continued to get. Every part of him wished he was in a crack den or busting a meth lab right now—anywhere but here.

He answered the phone and got Quast on the line.

# 51

CONference call

Diego and Farnsworth leaned towards the back of their display as Quast's tiny voice came through the speaker-phone.

"Maybe Miles can explain it better."

"Hey guys," the tech specialist's voice joined the line.

"What have you got for us?"

"Not much," said Miles. "But that, in and of itself, says something. If I couldn't find what I was looking for then it means that someone is trying to hide something."

He continued unchecked. "We looked into the *Knights of the Illuvian Age* Kickfunder and peeled back the veil to see if it was tied to Wheaton in any way beyond being another acting credit; if he was involved any deeper, it would indicate culpability. That's when we hit some roadblocks. The funds are all routed through some banks in countries that don't allow us to see who the accounts actually belong to. Those were banking haven countries and so their encryption was tougher than the standard American stuff."

"Typical Hollywood," Diego hissed. "Smoke and mirrors." He glared across the vendor's hall to Kubrick who still did brisk business on his end of the sales floor.

"Anything else to tell us, Miles?" Farnsworth asked.

"Just that this thing has made a crap-ton of cash so far. Also, with all these banks overseas, it might be possible that someone is planning to take the money and run."

"My thoughts exactly." A sour tint of pessimism bled into Diego's voice.

Farnsworth tapped his lips thoughtfully as Quast brought him up to speed with what she'd learned from Di Santo. "Henry Sheen was definitely not a comic book guy," she concluded after explaining how he'd made annual orders for comic books, regardless of that fact. "It seems material to the case."

"Before you go," Farnsworth asked, "Was it always the same time of year, or even day, that he bought comics on?"

"According to Di Santo, yes. He only remembered that it was in January. He'd marked it on a calendar each year."

Diego ended the call, but Farnsworth remained deep in thought. His eyes stayed locked on the Goblin Hole's owner while he pondered something.

"What was it you said Kubrick told you about where he got his comics from—the ones he started his business with?"

Diego's eyes narrowed to slits. "Basically that he inherited them, got them at garage sales, that kind of thing... found them in an attic, that's what he said. Do you think they could be forgeries?"

Farnsworth zoomed in on the man with his mobile phone and snapped a photo of his face. "No. That label on top of the comics' hard plastic cases show they've been graded and authenticated. Do you have a pic of Sheen on your phone?"

Diego pulled up the mugshot and handed the device to his partner who held the photos of Kubrick and Sheen side by side.

After a pause he deduced, "They're related."

Diego snatched both screens and compared. They did share some similar facial features.

"That's who he bought the comics for when he was in prison... Kubrick's probably his little brother. Henry would've known that his parents passed away while in witness protection. His comic subscription started before that, though. I think this was an annual gift to his kid brother." Farnsworth fired off a quick text to Miles asking for Casey Kubrick's birthday.

"And Witness Protection would explain why they have different names and a lack of any tangible connection between them. The feds scrubbed all their info before the Bratva trial over a decade ago after Sheen burned them."

Diego nodded with some amazement. "Pretty good hunch. Are you thinking Casey Kubrick knew about the money from the trial—the cash that Henry kept?"

"Reselling rare and expensive comics is a pretty good way to launder a couple million dollars." His phone chirped. "But it won't work for *hundreds* of millions."

Diego caught onto his train of thought. "But a multi-million dollar crowd funding campaign *is*."

"I think we have a solid lead." Farnsworth lifted his phone to show his partner Miles' text. It listed a birthday for Casey Kubrick as January 11.

The big detective glared at his enemy. Wil Wheaton walked over to the Goblin Hole and greeted the huge crowd of folks interested in the *Knights of the Illuvian Age* display. He snapped a few photos with the shyster director at his side.

"Should we arrest him?" Farnsworth asked.

"No." Diego's voice sounded resentful. "As long as we have eyes on him, we'll eventually find Sheen. More importantly, we've got to keep Wheaton safe from Houdek—as soon as the case breaks we lose that opportunity."

"That's more important than taking down McCloud's killer?"

Diego grimaced, but nodded. "I don't care if *we* bring them to justice or if Zmei does. It wouldn't bother me any if he kills Sheen, but it sounds like Wheaton is innocent... this is how McCloud would've wanted it."

Farnsworth and Diego both sat back in their chairs, maintaining their watch. Jessica approached from the distance. She'd apparently calmed down by now.

"How long has that guy been there?" Farnsworth spotted a man in a purple bunny fursuit purchasing an old book from a Mideastern man only a few booths away. The vendor gave him a subtle nod of the head.

"What guy?" Diego asked, scanning the booths.

Farnsworth looked again, but couldn't find the booth, as if it had disappeared... or never even existed in the first place. "Never mind. It must've been nothing," he said as he watched the purple rabbit exit the vendor hall while toting the heavy codex.

Jessica plopped down between them as if her earlier outburst had never happened. "What'd I miss?"

# 52

The Cake is a Lie

Clutching the arcane book to his chest, Sir Hops Alot bravely accompanied his furry crew of thirteen volunteers through the lobby. They keenly felt the squinty eyed glares of the nearby Bronies as they intermingled with the general menerderie within the public spaces.

One of their number led the crew, guided by a dousing rod made of cosplaying props. Grunkle Stan's cane and a lightsaber had been taped together to make the distinctive Y-shape; a Supernatural amulet hung purchased from a prop dealer from the end. It led them to a place where the barrier between worlds was weakest.

Sir Hops Alot opened the restroom door for he and his crew. They formed a cluster in the middle of the restroom as the divining sticks pointed to the floor.

A few random congoers milled about, obviously unnerved by the sudden influx of colorful fursuits in the men's room.

"Come on, come on. Hurry up," the purple rabbit muttered. "You." He pointed to the furry in the back. What's your name again?"

"Uh. Cat-boy... man," said the guy wearing a mostly lime-green, mismatched cat suit. Patches of duct tape barely held it together.

"Cat Boy Man, make sure nobody else comes through those doors."

"Meow," Cat Boy Man responded.

Sir Hops Alot stared impatiently at the few remaining outsiders there. Finally, he screamed with a blood-curdling shriek. That proved enough to push the remainder of the comparatively normal folk out the door.

The purple rabbit cracked open the Necronomicon and began following the detailed instructions. Using a bottle of ketchup they commandeered from the wiener vendor outside, he began drawing an eldritch circle on the floor and ringed it with arcane sigils. He hoped that whatever dark forces powered these rites wouldn't be too discerning over him using ketchup instead of goats' blood, but he just didn't have the stomach for that.

"Okay, everyone," Sir Hops Alot ordered his impromptu coven. "Stand here and chant with me. ph'nglui mglw'nafh Cthulhu R'lyeh wgah'nagl fhtagn." He whirled his arms to increase the cadence and volume. "ph'nglui mglw'nafh Cthulhu R'lyeh wgah'nagl fhtagn!" The air tingled and a foul wind blew through the tomb-like lavatory as Sir Hops Alot yelled the ineffable name; like a sorcerer of old he summoned the Great Old One aid them against their mortal enemies. "Nyarlathotep. By the power of the lords of R'lyeah... Zi Dinger Kia Kanpa! Zi Dingir Anna Kanpa! Zi Kia Kanpa! Zi Anna Kanpa! Aid us Nyarlathotep!"

The room seemed to tremble. Individual molecules began to buzz within the air and the floor split open in the center of the circle. The portal belched foul, noxious fumes and the air filled with screams as tentacles shot forth from it.

Scaly green appendages whirled and writhed across the room, seizing the furries and dragging them through the rift. The unseeing limbs busted porcelain and snapped water supplies, spraying in every direction.

As plumes of water splashed skyward, sending a thin mist through the air, trickles of mini-floods from each fixture spilled into the void, raining down into the alien dimension.

The bathroom door pushed open and an elderly, Asian man pushed a mop bucket and cleaning cart into the lavatory. His eyes widened as he got a full view of the trashing, alien tentacles.

"Nope," he said. He turned around and left.

Posting an Out of Order sign on the exterior of the door he put down a caution cone to deter anyone from checking it out. With a shrug, the custodian simply walked away.

Insert into Base

discard

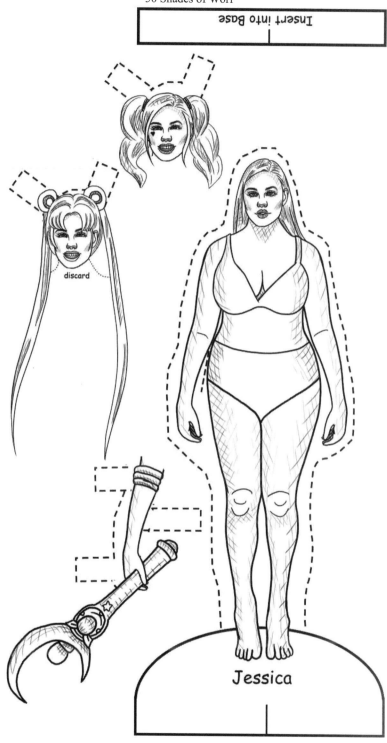

Jessica

Post pics of your weirdest scenes to
#50ShadesofWorf

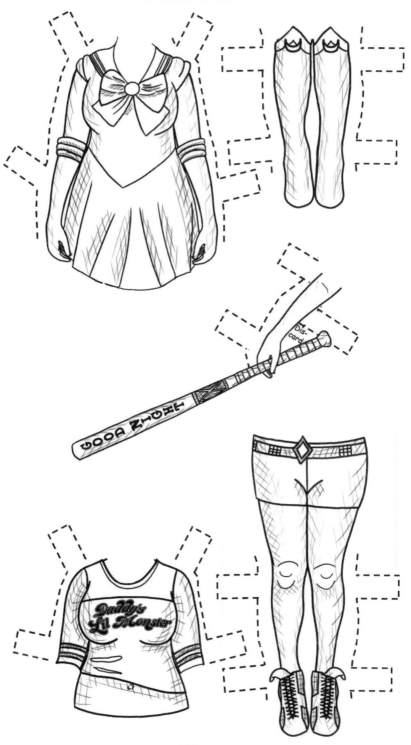

Post pics of your weirdest scenes to
#50ShadesofWorf

# PART SIX

## DAY 3

# 53

So It Begins

"I still don't understand why you couldn't go with an easier costume," Diego complained to Fansworth as they flashed their vendor badges and entered at the back of the convention center. "I mean, just put on a bath robe and be one of those Jedi things."

Farnsworth grinned beneath his light coat of airbrushed, red face-paint. "That was not the costume you were looking for," he said with a wave of his hand.

Diego arched an eyebrow, failing to understand. He simply shook his head. "I still feel like I'm gonna stick out like a sore thumb." Diego bundled up the edges of his crimson cape in order to both warm his bare top and keep it from snagging in the door. "I still don't get why mythology is suddenly a thing for you nerds."

"Leonides? The 300? Do you even *own* a television?" Farnsworth asked.

He shrugged. "I think we watch different programming."

"The Three Hundred was a hit comic before it was a movie, but ancient mythologies have always been a thing... lots of classic movie material, there. Just watch out for people screaming 'This is Sparta!' and trying to kick you in the gut."

Diego frowned, but so far Farnsworth's tips had come in handy. Still, Diego doubted many of the kids hopped up on sugary drinks had enough dexterity to kick higher than his waistline, let alone the gumption to try.

"Besides. You'll be fine as soon as we're inside... you won't feel as self conscious once there are others around in cosplay." He handed his partner a replica of Leonides's Spartan helmet.

"I hope you're right," he said. "If any time is best for Houdek to strike, it will be today." He held the prop in his hands and looked at the helmet. "How the heck am I supposed to see out of this thing? It covers most of my face."

"The human eye has a blindspot here and here," Farnsworth waved a hand by either side of Diego's face. "You don't actually see anything here—your brain fills in the missing data. It'll be fine; you'll see normally once you put it on and you'll never notice a difference."

He frowned skeptically but kept walking. They rounded a corner and stopped in their tracks.

Farnsworth looked away, hoping his disguise would throw off anyone who knew him and Diego pulled on his Spartan helmet to help hide his identity. Harding and two other guards sat in the detectives' sales space, waiting impatiently.

"Crap! I knew I forgot something," Diego muttered.

"What?"

"The print, the one the Confather demanded."

Farnsworth scowled, but there was nothing they could do, now.

"Okay. New plan, we'll have to loiter close to Wheaton."

As they entered the convention hall, the light source switched to fluorescent and Diego stopped, nearly busting a gut with laughter. "Who were you supposed to be again?"

"I told you a bunch of times. I'm Hellboy!" He stopped when he noticed his painted arms. "Ah crap! I shouldda known that would happen." Under the interior lights his thinly misted red paint presented as more of a lavender.

Farnsworth yanked out his smart phone and frantically scrolled for info. He dropped a bunch of curses and muttered, "Don't tell my mom I used sailor talk." His brow furrowed when he found an article. "Crap. It's called metamerism.

Apparently it's a thing with fluorescent light and certain pigments and dyes."

"Oh yeah," Diego said. "It's a thing alright."

Farnsworth stomped his hoof-like boots. "Let's hope nobody will notice."

"Don't worry. I'm not the pop culture junkie you are, but I can't think that purple Sea-biscuit was ever a thing."

Wearing his lavender scowl, Farnsworth led the way deeper inside as the convention opened. The dynamic duo strolled through a few rows of miscellaneous trinket vendors.

Booth babes hired by various non-comic related products kept ogling Diego's impressive, spartan physique. Farnsworth noticed that they kept distracting his partner as they searched for the best vantage of the crowd nearest Wheaton. The actor had just come out for an appearance in the VIP section; he had been promoting the *Knights of the Illuvian Age* panel to happen later.

Farnsworth cozied up to Diego as soon as the barely dressed model hired off of a Craigslist ad engaged his partner. The woman placed her hand on Diego's abs as if they were somehow relevant to the five-hour energy drinks she was pushing samples of.

The purple painted nerd laughed as if something were funny. He leaned over and brushed her hand away, pawing at Diego's bare chest. With his most effeminate lisp and a salacious wink he stated, "Hands to yourself, honey. This beefcake's all mine." He towed his partner from the scene as if he'd rescued Sir Galahad the Chaste from the Castle Anthrax.

Diego turned ashen. "What? Get your hand off of me," he said once they'd gotten away, pointing out that Farnsworth was still touching him.

"Sorry. Got carried away with the role-playing. Epic fail, huh?"

Finally they came upon a loose action figure vendor whose toys had all been setup in suspiciously inappropriate poses. The detectives started scanning the crowds, making a slow drift through the booths to seem less conspicuous.

Jessica popped out from behind one of displays. "Still at it, I see?" she asked. "Ohmygod... Farnsy, have you gone full Brony?"

Both detectives were engrossed in their surveillance and neither responded to her, although Farnsworth's silent treatment may have been mere spite for yesterday's outbursts.

Jessica crossed her arms and the bells on the two ends of her red and black Harley Quinn headgear jingled. She thumped Diego playfully with her over-sized hammer that said 'your face here' on one end of the mallet. "Hey. I get that you guys are here on police business, but, like, I totally witnessed a murder two days ago and nobody's handcuffed me yet or made me give a statement. Somebody better tell me what's going on here."

Diego barely glanced her way. "Sorry. Still top secret. We're still undercover for a day or so."

She stood straight as if a light bulb just went off in her head.

"Nice costume, though," Farnsworth said. "At least you went with the classy version of Harley Quinn instead of the slutty one again."

Diego shot back an intrigued look. "There's a slutty one... and *again*?"

"White shirt, booty shorts, pink and blue pigtails. It's pretty hot, just a little over-done, in my opinion."

Diego did his best to keep his face neutral.

Finally, Jessica broke. "I got in trouble at work. That colored hair dye doesn't come out of blond hair very well."

"What do you do?" Diego asked.

For all her previous candor, Jessica blushed.

"She teaches kindergarten," Farnsworth answered.

"Oh, like being a detective is so difficult," she hissed, perturbed that someone had spoken for her. "I've already figured out what you're doing. Someone killed a Wesley Crusher cosplayer; you say you're only under cover through today when Wil Wheaton is leaving after the *Knights of the Illuvian Age* panel; either you're planning to arrest him or someone is trying to murder Wil Wheaton."

She said that last bit a little too loudly for their comfort and both stepped closer to shush her.

"So I'm right?"

Diego looked at Farnsworth with a glare that instructed silence. He put a massive hand on either of Jessica's shoulders.

"Listen," she bartered, "either you can let me help you guys or I can go tell Wheaton the truth. Obviously you haven't told him about it or you'd be a whole lot closer to him than you are right now." She turned to Farnsworth. "I know we had a thing before. I'm over you and you're over me," she stuck out a hand to shake. "We're both adults and we can still be friends without any weirdness. This has nothing to do with old feelings... I just want to help. For realz."

Farnsworth looked sidelong at Diego, his lips thin and straight. He took her hand and shook it. "We gotta tell her," he told his partner.

"Fine." Diego told her, "You're right. We're protecting Wheaton from an assassin. Now, not a word," he demanded.

Jessica practically buzzed with excitement as she bounced up and down. "You won't regret this! I can help, really, I can." She jumped in and gave Farnsworth a big hug.

He tried to pry himself free, but another set of arms clamped down on him from behind, trapping him in the middle.

"Looks like a love sandwich," Deadpool said from behind Farnsworth. He leaned forward and whispered into his ear seductively, "Who's the meat?"

"Somebody kill me," Farnsworth begged.

"*You're* the meat," Deadpool said softly.

Diego continued his surveillance without interfering. "Hey, these are *your* people. *You* figure it out." He scanned the ever shifting flow of people before muttering an oft repeated mantra below his breath, "I really wish we knew what this guy looked like."

The over-the top anti-hero leaned in towards Farnsworth again and asked. "I love the Pegasus outfit. May I call you Peggy? Can you fly me to get my chimichangas?"

Farnsworth raised a purple eyebrow and before he realized it, Deadpool slapped a pair of cardboard, mini fairy wings onto his shoulders. "Wait! What? Dang it!" He tugged at them, but they wouldn't separate from his shirt. "Is… is this superglue?"

Deadpool laughed maniacally and nodded.

"I'm Hellboy, dammit!" Farnsworth screamed, "Hellboy!" he lunged towards the red-clad jokester, but Deadpool stuck his arms out, made airplane noises, and then flew away.

Farnsworth glared to his partner who shrugged. "I'm Hellboy," he slumped his shoulders, still insisting.

"Sure you are, partner."

# 54

The Confather Part III

Alan Tudyk, the venerable Confather, sat on his reconstructed throne and poured over the aged trifold brochure: the holy pamphlet. Long had it haunted his dreams. It predated even the Great Schism that divided the Brony and Furry factions... published even prior to the Marvel Cinematic Universe—it came from a time before nerds were ironically cool, ages before the first hipster crawled out from the primordial muck of the internet and twisted his first man-bun with the declaration of his, hers, or its full frontal nerdity.

The clip-art heavy brochure was little more than an invitation to join a cult. Nobody really knew if it had ever been more than a joke, but it had taken on a holy-text-like status among the two groups.

A proto-Furry named Green Mittens, the author of the text, had long since disappeared from the scene. Rumors were either that he had married a Normal, settled down in the suburbs and had kids, or that he had died in some horrific outbreak of necrotizing fasciitis that had mutated within his fursuit. So basically the same fate.

The Confather ignored the comic sans text that attempted to recruit people into the cult. Instead, he focused on the simple drawings watermarked behind the lettering: the source of the prophecy.

Crude images drawn mostly in crayon, and seemingly by Napolean Dynamite, adorned the foldout. Animal people gathered on one side and on the other were colorful pony folk; between them stood a smiling man-horse with tiny wings; his arms stretched out to both groups as his tiny sword fell from his hands, possibly as a sign of peace depending on which theologian was consulted.

Tudyk knew there had to be answers in the pamphlet somewhere. He'd heard whisperings of a new, detailed image, but the two con-goers that he'd sent after the piece had failed to deliver it. He needed to do everything he could to keep his clandestine kingdom together—at least until Joss Whedon got off his rear end and decided to give his fans another Firefly project. In the meanwhile, the Bronies and Furries threatened to tear apart everything that he had worked so hard for.

Pink Panther sat impatiently at the negotiation table and Tudyk walked around him. He gave him a wide berth; the con crud had already begun to ripen and the fursuit smelled like a Taco Bell inspired cologne.

One of the Confather's guards arrived, flanked by a pudgy, hispanic twenty-something. The stranger brushed his turquoise hair from his face with a set of manicured, rainbow painted nails. He glared at the costumed man opposite him. Pink Panther's body language suggested that he was doing the same from behind his mask.

"Gentle-beings," the Confather greeted in a firm voice. Tudyk tried to put a husky tone into it. "You know who I am?"

They both nodded. "Yes, Confather," said the Brony whose name on the VIP badge identified him only as Pleasure Magic.

"I have called you here to negotiate a…" he started coughing from the tickle in his throat and switched back to his normal voice with a hard swallow. "I've called you here to negotiate a new peace between you."

"Peace?" Pleasure Magic guffawed. "*They* know nothing of peace."

They immediately began bickering.

Tudyk hollered over them, but they paid no heed. Finally, he turned and kicked over his throne, bursting the duct tape seams and sending a spray of carbonated nectar all across the floor.

Both leaders shut up immediately.

"Listen! I cannot have your people's age-old grudge disturbing the convention. I've got enough other problems without a furry civil war breaking out."

Pink Panther guffawed, "You think *you* can stop that? No. This is war. And the only one who can stop it now is the Chosen One of prophecy."

Pleasure Magic hissed. "So its war you want?"

"Hey! Knock it off," Tudyk stood and threatened them with his imposing, average physique. "I'm not kidding around. Either we work something out or there's going to be consequences." He snatched both of their badges.

Their eyes widened in terror. "You wouldn't dare kick us out. If we don't return from a peaceful parley, our tribes will certainly go to war!"

The Confather threw the badges in the trash. "Fine! Then the outcome is the same either way, but *my* way has one less idiot to worry about on each side." He nodded his head and security came and took them by the arms in order to escort them from the premises.

Suddenly, the doors burst open and a lime green furry tumbled to his hands and knees. Soaked head to toe, a third of his costume had been shredded and fresh wounds marked his exposed skin. He scampered to Tudyk and clung to his legs.

"Jeffrey? I was wondering where you'd gone off to."

"I did it, cousin! I infiltrated them like you asked... But I... I saw things. *Dark, strange things.*" He visibly shook. Jeffrey whispered, "Things I'll never unsee..."

"What is it, Jeffrey?"

"There is no Jeffrey—not anymore. My transformation is complete. I am Cat Boy Man, now."

"He's one of them!" Pleasure Magic howled.

"How dare you spy on us," Pink Panther accused.

"Get them out of my con." Tudyk yelled.

"I'm telling Tumblr!" Pleasure Magic screamed as they dragged him from the throne room.

"Aw! C'mon guys. Not Tumblr! What can I do to stop this stupid war?" Tudyk called after them.

"Only the Chosen One can stop it now!" they both screamed, finally agreeing on something.

After several long moments and eight tiny, sample bottles of UV taken from a vendor as tribute, Cat Boy Man told him all about the arcane portal ripping a breach through time and space in the men's restroom. His eyes and hair had both nearly turned white from terror.

"I must've been on the other side for years—at least it felt like it. None of the others made it; I am the lone survivor." He handed his cousin a circular, jade artifact etched with a seven pointed star. "Take this. Only this seal can close the dimensional portal. You must stop the dreaded Nyarlathotep."

Tudyk turned it over in his hands. "Aw crap. This was the *last* thing I needed." He pointed to the remaining security guard. "Go and round up some Stargate SG-1 cosplayers or something and bring them to the bathroom. Oh… and bring along anyone dressed like someone from Twilight, too."

"Twilight?"

"Yeah. Especially any Robert Pattison kinda guys—really, any sparkling vampires will do.

He raised an eyebrow.

Tudyk sighed. "I've actually seen this before, at a con in Florida. There's a toilet that leads straight into hell. The Twilight kids are just in case they run into Cthulu, I know that he generally prefers a snack before being put back to sleep."

The soldier nodded. "I understand." He saluted like a Spaceball and whirled around to leave, finding the door on only his second try.

# 55

Mike and Sulley Find the Nudie LEGOs

The two detectives scanned each and every person that came or went. "What about that guy?" Farnsworth often asked, not quite sure why he'd picked a man from the crowd and unable to narrow down exactly what intangibles made an individual feel out of place.

Diego shook his head and checked his watch. Finally he glanced back at Kubrick and the Goblin Hole booth. A tall cosplayer in a black hood and robe leaned over the kiosk's counter when the owner was distracted and reached into Kubrick's satchel. He swiped a few unseen items before moving on.

Shaking his head, Diego almost chuckled. He knew in his gut that Kubrick was dirty and somehow tied to this whole conspiracy, probably even more than they'd discovered so far. It pleased him somewhat to see the greedy masses nickle and diming him, even if it was probably only for tickets to an exclusive convention panel.

Diego yawned. They'd been at it for hours and regularly shifted positions to try and allay suspicion from the booth jockeys who they made regular eye contact with. He checked his clock; they were running out of time, and by all accounts, this assassin never missed.

"I gotta take a leak, quick," Diego said. "You keep an eye on the prize."

He hurried towards the lobby and found a small crowd loitering outside of the bathroom where a "Do Not Enter" sign had been hung. Some kind of fetid liquid had leaked from beneath the door. It looked like radiator fluid but smelled like rotting corpses.

Diego scowled at the bathroom where a collection of men and women wearing respirators cut a line through the crowd. They wore a style of military uniform that he couldn't recognize. More than half of them were apparently named O'Neill.

He watched them steel themselves and then breach the door. Diego turned when another watcher commented, "Looks like a 2319, right?"

The detective turned and found a man who wore a kind of yellow hazmat suit with goggles propped up on his head. "Like, from Monsters Inc?" Diego asked.

"Yeah, buddy," the yellow stranger said. "You really know your stuff—that's almost an obscure reference nowadays!"

Diego shrugged. "Well, I have a niece who is four." He looked at the man in the yellow suit and pointed. "Minion, right?"

The stranger wrinkled his nose with seeming disbelief. "No... Walter White!"

Diego shrugged.

"Breaking Bad?"

"Whatever. I've gotta piss."

The talkative stranger pointed the way to the next nearest lavatory and Diego left the whole odd scene behind.

Back in the vendor hall, Wheaton abruptly stood during a signing with some fans and grabbed the bat'leth that had been mounted on a rack behind Dorn. The older actor tried to slap the younger actor's hand away, but Wheaton outmaneuvered him. He snatched the very real weapon and began spinning it around with a cocky kind of showmanship.

Dorn and Wheaton began arguing and shoving each other like overgrown children on a playground. The convention's celebrity handler tried to intervene but failed to break up the impromptu wrestling match.

Farnsworth and Jessica watched while trying to move beyond the stakeout post that they'd held for too long. "I dunno," she said. "I really think Dorn *wants* to kill him. But can you really hold it against him?"

"I don't think so," he said watching her as she awkwardly traced the shape of Michael Dorn's body with her hands, despite the distance.

"Well, *I'd* like to hold it *against him*," she said lasciviously and bit her lower lip seductively. "Maybe I could get a Trekking to Remember? I wouldn't mind me some Fifty Shades of Worf. I already have a costume to match," she giggled.

Distracted by such spontaneous lewdness, Farnsworth bumped into an overweight shopper who carried a tall stack of knock-off LEGO kits. The boxes of custom pieces tumbled to the floor.

An eight year old pointed and laughed at a particular box with a nude LEGO man. The kid laughed and read the text bubble. "Ha ha! 'Where are my pants?'" He pointed to the other, female custom minis. "And where are *her* pants?" The child's mother quickly dragged him away.

"Jeez, man. What? Is this your first con or something?" The portly pervert rasped, out of breath from rushing to pick up his stack of naked, plastic treasures. Quickly, he hid the adult themed interlocking plastic brick kit that featured a "build your own BDSM dungeon" on the bottom. He didn't get to it quickly enough and flashed the "six included flesh-painted mini-figures" to all of the nearby shoppers.

He stood and hurried off, desperately trying not to make eye contact with anyone while he muttered something about his NSFW purchase being for research.

Farnsworth paused, suddenly introspective. He blurted, "I've figured it out!"

Jessica grudgingly pulled her eyes away from her Klingon man-crush DaSjaj. "Really? Naked LEGOs unraveled your mystery?"

Farnsworth shook his head. "I know who we need to be searching for... we keep wondering how we're going to find Gage Houdek, the Bratva hitman, but we're looking for someone who we don't have a description for while just hoping that he'll somehow be self-evident."

"So?" asked Jessica. "Shouldn't he be?"

"What do you notice about all of the folks here at the con?"

"Well, it's day three, so... the general odor?"

"Close," Farnsworth explained. "You're on the right track. You're right that all the regulars seem to have certain things in common: they walk around like they own the place and nobody pays attention tothe weird, little things like the smell or random absurdities that outsiders haven't learned to appreciate."

Jessica gave him a screwed up look.

"Okay. Let me ask you a question. Could you, with just a few seconds of observation, tell a n00b from a seasoned regular?"

"Heck yes. Leet baby." She went for a high-five and Farnsworth awkwardly gave it to her. "1337!"

"Okay," Farnsworth asked, "why?"

Jessica paused, dumbfounded. "I don't know. I can't quite explain it... just a general sense, I guess. Probably a collection of all the little things, like their reactions to things, not knowing how to act, weird responses to things that are generally considered normal at cons."

"Exactly! Could someone fake it, and could you tell?"

"I think they *could,* but I also think that I could tell. I've been to a lot of cons. There are too many little things... body language maybe, I think he or she would probably overcompensate. I don't know. But seasoned eyes don't lie."

Farnsworth grinned enthusiastically. "That's how we're going to find Zmei."

A light seemed to ding above Jessica's head. "By looking for first-timers?"

He nodded. "And Rick, Detective Diego, should be able to guess if someone is our man once we narrow down the initial suspects."

Jessica's brow furrowed. "I don't think you can just *teach him how to tell the difference.*"

"Nope. That's why you'll have to point those people out to him. I'll stay here and watch for anybody who gets near Wheaton or Kubrick."

"But... he's in the bathroom."

Farnsworth squinted at her. "Since when has that ever stopped you before."

Her eyes popped. "Yeah. You're right!" Jessica started to leave and then paused for some reassurance. "I'm just checking that you're not messing with me. Neither of you two are gay, right? I mean, totally fine if you are... just don't mess with me and pull the carrot away later."

"No! Now just go find him! The *Knights of the Illuvian Age* panel is in less than two hours, and Houdek is, in all likelihood, already here, somewhere."

# 56

Eagle Eye

"Aren't you a little short for a Darth Vader?" a costumed man with black leather and metal claws asked a Star Wars cosplayer.

Behind a mask, the armored, lightsaber wielding person responded in a female's voice, "Aren't you a little fat for a Wolverine?" she jabbed back.

Wolverine blanched and put a hand over his heart. "Oh my glob. Hurts... so... much. No healing factor can keep up with that."

Vader removed her helmet and winked at the X-man. "That's okay. I like em a little bigger. Cuddly guys try harder, if you know what I mean." She linked an arm through his and they walked off.

Jessica jabbed an elbow into Diego's ribs. "That was like, the perfect love story!"

The detective continued scanning the crowd. "Hmm, what?"

"You didn't even see it."

"Sorry. Trying to prevent a murder over here. Aren't you supposed to be helping?"

"Oops. Shiny objects." Jessica started scanning the crowd again as she twirled her over-sized wooden mallet.

"How about that guy?" Diego asked, pointing to a man wearing every day clothing.

The suspect turned.

"No way. Those clothes are from the eighties... and that hat?"

Diego asked, "So?"

"He's in costume. Clearly he's Dustin from Stranger Things. But yeah, he might be a first timer." She stood on her toes. "But what about that guy behind him?"

A man wearing a suit walked through the aisle as if on a mission. He held a bolt of black cloth draped over his forearm like a concierge.

"Never mind. I think he's with convention center hospitality."

"No," Diego disagreed and began immediately moving to follow nonchalantly. "He's not wearing a name tag."

Jessica hurried after the detective. "You really think this could be our guy?"

Diego slipped between the con-goers and pursued. He nodded and put a finger to his lips to shush her. "He's tailing someone—this is bad. I think we have our guy," he checked a clock on the wall of the lobby as they cut across the horde of mismatched mythologies.

"Right. Like in the movies... police can always tell when somebody is following them, right?"

"It's a cop thing," Diego grinned, scanning back and forth. He'd somehow lost his visual on the guy when they had to sidestep a gigantic, green gorilla wearing a tie and a name tag that read Dank-ey Kong. The stoned age gorilla tried to get anyone within arm's reach to follow him on social media.

A nearby group of red-shirted Trekkies suddenly collapsed like they were part of some dork-driven flash mob. All attention turned to the actors who'd just faked a spontaneous massacre. A child in their midst wore a Storm Trooper Halloween costume and looked very confused by what had just happened.

"I guess that answers that question," a woman said nearby.

Beyond the mob of prone red shirts, Diego spotted a service hallway door slowly closing on its hydraulic assist. "There," he pointed and pursued.

The suited man stepped back into view. Opening the door, Gage Houdek slipped into the corridors in pursuit of his mysterious quarry.

"I don't know who he's chasing," Diego said, "but hopefully the hallways are friendlier this time around or I swear to God I'm going to shoot a furry."

Jessica put a hand on his bicep. "Maybe there's an easier way. If he's here, he had to have purchased admission, right? They make everyone provide personal contact information in order to get in. Maybe you could get his ID and then call in the calvary?"

Diego paused, and then shook his head. "He's surely got access to fakes."

Nearby a man in only his underwear thrashed as security hauled him towards the exit. Waving a plastic, prop sword, he raved like a lunatic, "*I am the Witch-King of Angmar!* I'm telling you... someone *stole* my con badge! Look me up in the system—I was a VIP! He took my costume and *everything! I was VIP!*"

The man's escort gave him no heed as they dragged the wailing theft victim towards the doors like a team of sled dogs.

Jessica shrugged, acknowledging the point was moot as they arrived at the hallway door just before it could click shut.

Detective Rick Diego braced himself and sucked in a lungful of air and held it. If it was anything like he expected on day three of a con, those sweaty fursuits would make him wish he'd brought an air tank from his SCUBA gear.

# 57

Dead End

Jessica yelped and clamped a hand over her mouth to stifle a scream as they got to the relative middle of corridor network.

A headless body lay splayed out in the middle of the floor. Blood leaked and pooled all around the body, but there was no sign of his murderer

It appeared that somebody hadn't appreciated this Deadpool cosplayer's particular brand of antics.

"Over there," Jessica pointed, "by the condensation pump." A severed, hooded head lay on its ear five feet away, nestled between used coolant parts.

Diego swallowed the thick feeling in his throat; Houdek had killed again. He raised an eyebrow at Jessica's use of the damaged equipment's terminology.

"I used to be married to a refrigeration repair tech… happily divorced five years, now."

The sharp and gory smell of iron intermingled with the ethyl odors produced by the abandoned freezer parts they'd smelled the last time through.

Diego knelt over the body and checked him for any identification but he came up clean. His convention badge only listed him as Deadpool. One of the cosplayer's swords, bloody and with a cocked and broken handle, had been dropped against the wall several paces further.

"Is—is that how he…"

The Detective nodded. "I don't know why Houdek would've been chasing this guy, though. But it is possible. Houdek's the kind of lunatic that goes out of his way to kill people that make him mad… chopped the guy's head clean off and with his own sword." The blade was of no value after one use, like most cheaply made, decorative weapons, the metal blunted easily and the handle had been designed to break on sharp impact.

Diego retrieved a tube of paper that had been stowed next to one of the character's blade sheaths. He unrolled it and found the print of the S&M pegasus that had become so desirable for reasons unknown to him. It marked the deceased as the same man they had met before and Diego almost understood why Houdek would kill him.

After rolling the print back up, he passed the artwork to Jessica before checking the rest of the scene. Scouting the rest of the hall, he couldn't find any trace of the assassin.

Frustration was not difficult to spot on his face, though equal parts of worry seemed to contend for shelf space. "Go bring that print to security and tell them that the Confather asked for it. They will get it where it's supposed to go, as if it even matters anymore." He checked the time. "There's only a half hour before the *Illuvian Age* panel, anyway."

She nodded. The ends of her pig-tailed headpiece jingled. "And what about you?"

"I'm going to poke around the hallway a little more… but I've got to call this one in. We're running out of time and if we haven't found Houdek by now, Wil Wheaton's as good as dead if we don't."

Jessica wrapped the graphic art around the thick pole of her giant mallet and tightened her grip to keep it together. "Be careful, big guy," she insisted and then blew him a kiss.

# 58

Noodle Service

Farnsworth kept his vigil over Wil Wheaton.

The actor kept his feud against his one-time costar alive. He'd started folding paper footballs made from the programming guides and urged his fans to "kick field-goals" with them as they arrived for photo-ops; Michael Dorn was the target.

A man with a hospitality cart pushed his way through the aisle offering cups of instant ramen noodles and soda to any who cared for a pick-me-up. Everyone knew how much anime fans loved their ramen noodles and even though Maruchan decided not to sponsor the complimentary noddle service again this year, an entire pallet of noodles only cost about twenty bucks.

The cart drew a sizable crowd that blocked Farnsworth's view of the celebrities so he walked around the hive of sodium and villainy to keep an eye on things. He used the opportunity to grab some sustenance while the opportunity availed itself.

"Sorry for the warm soda, everybody," the convention employee said robotically. "Our refrigerators have been down for a while, now."

"Blech, the water is lukewarm, too?" a lady complained.

"We're making due," the man stated, "the Convention Center's commissary is torn apart for repairs. It just takes a few extra minutes for the noodles to soften."

An old man dressed as Dragon Ball's Master Roshi boldly proclaimed with the character's distinct inflection, "*I* know how to soften a noodle like nobody's business!"

The staffer rolled his eyes, likely making note to call in sick this time next year.

Farnsworth's ears perked up when he heard someone mentioning the back hallways. He tried to take a step closer, but the top of Farnsworth's pointy Hellboy tail had somehow gotten snagged on the cart. He gave it a tug and the appendage tore.

The detective cursed his luck beneath his breath and grabbed the prop piece. The rope-like fabric it had been made from began to unravel and fray. He shook his head with disgust; not every costume came together as well as the next, but his Hellboy had been a disaster.

Farnsworth slurped his tepid noodles before they were ready and closed the gap towards two bronies. Each sported a black eye they'd earned during the recent conflicts with the furries. They paid him no more mind than a single glance—though his outfit may have misled them into think he was one of their own.

"...apparently *everyone* thinks they can come and go as they please in our hallways, now," the one said. "Like they don't understand that the Confather gave them to us in the Mithril Hall act of 2013."

The second one grimaced. "And that weird guy with his buddy all tied up and ball-gagged? Yeah, there's *some* of that, but it was some straight up kinky stuff—normies don't understand that *that* isn't what we're all about."

Farnsworth tried to play off his lavender-skinned cover and approached them. "Someone took a hostage into the hallways?" He risked a glance back to make sure that both Kubrick and Wheaton were still safe at their booths.

"Yeah," one responded. "He wasn't one of us and he wasn't dressed like a furry."

"Maybe a *naked* furry," his friend interrupted.

"Anyway—it was totally strange. Dragged the poor guy by a rope. Musta been some crazy, weird fantasy or something. It wouldda been a lot less strange if he would've been wearing a Deadpool mask or even just a Punisher shirt... and I mean *just a Punisher shirt*."

"Where the heck *is* Deadpool anyway? I haven't seen him all day—he was supposed to bring me lunch." The brony looked around and spotted three Deadpool cosplayers in poorly constructed costumes happily insulting other con-goers. "The *real* Deadpool," he clarified.

Farnsworth understood what he meant. The man in question was likely the cosplayer he and his partner had run into already.

His friend shrugged and checked his Hello Kitty wristwatch. "Look at the time. We've gotta go get in line for the *Knights of the Illuvian Age* panel."

The other brony pounded a fist into his palm. "Yeah. Time for the purge!"

"Where in the halls did you see this guy—the hostage thing?" Farnsworth asked.

The bronies gave him a rough estimate. "Say... you look kinda familiar. Aren't you..."

"Nope, I'm Hellboy." Farnsworth cut him off and then dashed towards the nearest hallway access he could find. His fraying tail flapped behind him.

As soon as he hit the door he fired off a quick text to his partner. *Zmei is in the building! He's in the service tunnels—I know where...*

# 59

The Eye of the Con

"Captain Murphy—it's Diego. Listen, we've gotta shut this whole convention down!" Diego barked into his phone.

"What in the heck are you talking about?" Murphy snapped. "This had better not be about that guy who keeps calling the precinct complaining that someone stole his costume and swiped his entrance badge."

"No. Captain. Listen to me…"

"Good. Now *you* listen, we've been getting the same crank call from the Convention Center all day from a guy claiming to us he was stripped naked and thrown out. I don't know what kinda animal house they have set up over there, but I've got half a mind to slap the fools running TrollCon with a nuisance bill for tying up all our dispatchers."

"Houdek is here!" he blurted, "And I can't seem to find him. One bystander was found dead already and he gave me the slip. Wil Wheaton is about to take stage—he'll be at his most vulnerable right before then."

"Well you better find him, *and hurry!* I know Chief Cooper is planning on being in the front row for some big movie reveal event that they're doing this afternoon."

"Yeah," Diego gasped. "That's the event. We can't let it happen—I need as many officers as you can send. I have maybe twenty minutes."

A brief, silent moment filled the air.

"You haven't seen the news at all, today, have you?" More silence. Murphy continued. "Some wacko religious group is protesting. Decided to steal a page from the civil unrest playbook and marched into the streets and highway to block traffic. We've got every uniformed unit already on the streets trying to sort things out... idiots caused pileups a mile long. Half a dozen of em got run over and they plastered an entire overpass with blood-soaked evangelism tracts and littered the streets with pamphlets designed to look like hundred dollar bills. Right now, we barely have storm sewers working... the entire infrastructure is on shaky legs. I got ten officers alone responding to local counterfeit claims from street kids using em to buy candy and nudie mags."

"So what are you saying?"

"You're on your own. Even if I *had* officers to spare, they'd never be able to get through the tangled mess that surrounds you. You're at the center of a perfect storm."

Diego spat a string of curses and hung up. He and Farnsworth would not be getting backup. It was time to improvise.

His mobile chirped and vibrated with an incoming message from his partner. Farnsworth claimed he knew where Houdek was.

"Finally, some good news," he muttered.

# 60

Laus Stan Lee Aeternum

Flashes of eerie, green light strobed and frightened away any attendees standing near the quarantined men's room. A cushion of space opened up as con-goers shrank away from the foul, eldritch aura released into the world by the profane, trickster god of the men's room.

Only one man stood before the door, unwilling to yield even an inch of ground to Lovecraft's demons. Alan Tudyk called out to his team on the other side of the door.

"How's it going in there, you guys?"

One of the SG1 cosplayers hollered back. "We're almost there! Young O'Neill's got the amulet—we just have to…"

A blood curdling scream split the air followed by a grotesque gurgle.

"Guys? Guys, what do you have to do?"

Someone else's voice. "We have it back… so much blood! Fat O'Neill's got the amulet, now. Does anyone know how to speak Akkadian? Skinny O'Neill?"

The Confather grinded his teeth nervously. More howls of pain filled the air on the other side of the restroom door.

An excited convention goer, sure this was some sort of demonstration, used a cellphone to zoom in on the restroom's door where the out of order sign hung. "What's going on in there?" she asked Tudyk.

"Oh, nothing," he gave his best fake laugh and internally questioned his own acting ability. "Those are just plumbers in there. Little problem... there was a taco truck on the street yesterday. Soooo..."

An etheral cloud of malachite suddenly hissed from beneath the door and rushed across floor, coating the convention center in a sickly mist.

The door muffled those voices within the bathroom, but Tudyk stood close enough to hear them. "You—other O'Neill, draw the elder sign. The amulet! Smash it. *Smash it now!*"

"No! We'll be trapped—aaiiee... they're coming through— one got away—do it now before anything else gets to the gate!"

The mist suddenly rippled with electricity as it crawled and wreathed between the feet of all the con-goers. The crowd stood with eyes glued to the lavatory door. With a sudden wooshing, sucking sound, the mist and flashing energy pulled back into the bathroom.

A tense silence followed. The entire lobby held its collective breath.

Tudyk rushed ahead and peeked inside the door. The place was trashed. Water leaked everywhere and the fixtures had been annihilated, but the portal had closed.

The Confather checked his watch and frowned. There was no sign of the men and women who gave their all to save them and there was no time to look for them. Perhaps he would erect a small plaque here at next year's convention.

He glanced one more time at the devastation. What was done was done and Tudyk didn't want to begin meddling with any sort of dark arcana... not again. He'd made himself that promise long ago. Nothing remained now except to get to the *Knights of the Illuvian Age* panel and put out the next fire.

Tudky emerged from the bathroom door with a sigh of relief and took down the out of order sign. The crowd gathered in the lobby began cheering and applauding. Stunned, he stood a little straighter at the accolades.

Deadpool closed the door from the service hallway and put his head back on. The faint, green aura that glowed around him quickly faded away as he shook his head and cleared the momentary haze that resulted from the recent decapitation.

He coughed a few times until he'd cleared the last of the green mist from his lungs.

"Hey readers—why the heck are we clapping?" Deadpool said aloud and to nobody in particular. He slapped his hands together and whistled like a maniac at a sports event. "Yay! I'm included," he cheered.

The Confather took a bow and welcomed the people's applause. He lied, "Thank you! Thank you. That was just a little teaser for an upcoming project I'm working on with Nathan Fillion." People cheered extra hard for Fillion and Tudyk cursed under his breath. "No questions, please... just keep your eyes peeled for upcoming news."

He hurried towards the main hall where Wil Wheaton had been scheduled to unveil the first details for the new Kickfunder film to a rabid TrollCON audience. It was where he expected further anarchy to erupt between the warring furry and brony factions.

Alan Tudyk knew that he needed a miracle. He bowed his head and closed his eyes, praying to the mighty Stan Lee for exactly that.

"Dear Stan Lee... I know we haven't spoken much lately... not since the dark times—after Firefly was canceled—but you know that I'm in great need. I need your superhuman power to help stop the war that is coming... a war far greater than any DC and Marvel crossover event. Well, you know, in your omniscience. Give me the tools I need to save the Coniverse... the Unicon... the... things and stuff. Amen"

He opened his eyes and found Officer Harding standing in front of him with a busty woman in her too-tight Harley Quinn costume. She held out a rolled up piece of paper.

"I think this is what you've been searching for?"

Greedily he unfurled the paper and revealed the NSFW art print. "The prophecy," he whispered.

# 61

Chill Out (In An Arnold Voice)

Diego hung up his phone and spat profanity at the nearby wall. Footsteps echoed down the hall; with his nerves ratcheted so high, he pulled out his handgun which he'd concealed beneath his crimson cape.

He half expected the furries or bronies, but Farnsworth walked through the hallway. Diego lowered his weapon and gave a short whistle.

Farnsworth spotted him and hurried over. "You got my message?"

Diego nodded, not addressing the fact that the halls had turned uncannily silent. "Lead the way. You said you could find Houdek?"

The shorter detective sniffed the air and read the sign panels adorning the walls. "There's a kitchen around here for caterers and food services to use."

"Yeah," Diego said curtly. He pointed. "I already checked it out. It's all shut down, padlocked."

"Exactly. They have big walk in freezers and they're broken down right now! That's why they're closed."

Diego furrowed his brow.

"Didn't you ever flip burgers as a teenager? Those coolers are usually insulated and practically soundproof... I mean, not that I know, but I remember hearing stories about *other* kids hooking up in them. The cooling systems are down so it's the perfect place for a bad guy to hide."

"Maybe even hide a body?" Diego turned to sneak back towards the coolers and then paused. "Wait a minute... in the coolers? *Where they keep the food?* That's disgusting."

"Yeah. Totally gross," Farnsworth nodded and tried to play it off as cool.

Diego led the way to the commissary.

Farnsworth blushed and continued, "I'm so glad that sort of thing never happened to me. I would have hated that."

With a super serious look on his face the costumed spartan said, "That's one Whopper of a story." The padlock on the commissary doors had been cut since he'd last been here.

"Yeah," Farnsworth grinned. "Let's not even talk about the nuggets."

Diego put a finger to his lips as they drew closer to the chef's stations. The pair skulked through the shadows like ringwraiths.

A muffled sound permeated the air, like a far off scream.

Farnsworth pointed up to the ceiling. A ventilation shaft vibrated with the faint echoes of someone in pain. They traced the ductwork back towards the rear of the giant, walk-in freezer.

Diego adjusted the pistol in his grip and looked for a door. He shot Farnsworth a quizzical look; he couldn't find the freezer door.

Farnsworth joined in the search, but came up empty. He stepped back out the door and read the room's label. *Catering Service.*

"It's not the kitchen," he whispered, spotting something across the room. "This room is for prep and setup for caterers who bring in all their food from off-site."

Diego furrowed his brow, confused, when Farnsworth motioned him over to the wall where freezer parts laid haphazardly strewn across the floor as a sign of the ongoing repairs.

Farnsworth outlined the panel where a gridded vent leaned. He slowly peeled it back and moved the greasy cooling machinery aside so he could lay down and access the opening. It wasn't quite big enough to crawl though.

After he parted the hanging sheaves of fiberglass insulation, the pained groans came through all the louder. Farnsworth motioned for his partner to lay down and join him.

A musty odor of old thaw greeted them. Just beyond the immobile, steel blades of the cooling fan, they could see into the bottom section of the freezer. The door on the far side exited into a different kitchen other than the one they were in.

Four legs of a chair were visible with two human feet duct-taped to them and a rubber ball gag laid on the tile between them. Blood had trickled down and pooled on the floor.

"I already said I'd tell you whatever you wanted—I'll give it back—I'll give it *all back!*" the voice shrieked. His feet trembled and shook with another bout of screaming as someone, Houdek most likely, tortured the man.

Diego recognized the voice. He mouthed to his partner, *Henry Sheen.*

"You've been a busy boy," Houdek said with such a mild disinterest that it came across as eerie. "Killing cops and stealing from the Bratva."

Farnsworth cocked his head when he first heard the assassin's deep voice.

"It wasn't me," Sheen yelled frantically. "I mean, half of it was, and I can get you the money, but it was my brother, Casey! He's got it all—this was his idea."

Houdek's feet stopped their confident pacing as Sheen gave up his flesh and blood so readily. "You think it's as easy as that? Just give back the money and all is forgiven? After the Brotherhood gave you so much? Even if it *was* so simple, you killed a cop in the Bratva's backyard and brought down all manner of unnecessary heat. No, the Bratva only calls in Zmei when they've made up their minds... when there is no room for forgiveness."

"It was all Casey!" Henry shouted. "He set that up—a couple rattle cans and a cutting torch. I just supplied the camera and equipment. He had the whole thing planned out for years while I was doing my dime for the Brotherhood... something from some stupid comic book."

Diego stiffened as they eavesdropped. His fists clenched, but he remained silent.

"I went to *prison* for them," Henry argued.

"Yes, and now you have to die for them."

The detectives could hear Houdek playing with his signature butterfly knife as he walked predatory circles around the prisoner. *Click. Clack.* Sheen's breaths came in heavy, wet gasps. *Click. Clack.*

"It was not hard to figure out your whole plan: steal from the mob and launder the cash through a crowd funder. It sounds like a victim-less crime, almost, but there *are* victims—my employer. Any idiot can figure it out. Even the cops have already figured it out, and if *they're* sniffing close, any window of grace you may have had is closing." *Click. Clack.*

Sheen latched onto whatever carrots Houdek cared to dangle. "Tell me what I have to do to make it right," he implored.

"Oh, it's not what *you* can do." *Click. Clack.* "I was hired to do a job, and I *always* complete them. I'm gonna kill anyone and everything associated with this phony movie. The actors, the director, and everyone who pledged more than a token payment to make it happen." *Click. Clack.*

Farnsworth gulped so hard it was almost audible. He pointed at himself with his thumb.

*Click. Clack.* "Maybe it's not too late. I haven't marked Casey *Sheen*, yet. Perhaps seeing you like this will persuade him to do the right thing and return what he took from my employers... along with a sizable interest payment... like the extra money he swindled for this movie and the rare and expensive comics he purchased with the original cash you skimmed before doing your dime?"

All of the sudden, Houdek clacked his knife shut. "Look at the time. I've got to go and kill a certain celebrity, special request of the mob. You'd better hope that your brother is willing to give me what I want… for *his* sake. Maybe I just kill Casey *Kubrick* and let Casey *Sheen* live. Kubrick owes a lot of people a lot of money… and these people are far less forgiving than *me*."

A few seconds later, the heavy freezer door clanked shut and silence ruled, only broken up by the intermittent sobs of the imprisoned ex-con.

# 62

Arrested Developments

Farnsworth and Diego hurried into the hallway with guns drawn. The spartan whirled, covering the different angles; in the utility lighting, Farnsworth's painted skin matched the color shade of Diego's cape. There was no sign of the assassin.

"Come on," Diego hissed and set his eyes forward.

Farnsworth stepped the opposite direction as his partner, towards the short corridor that would lead to the kitchen access. "But we have to get Sheen."

Diego's eyes narrowed to slits. "He's not going anywhere."

"We're going to need him," Farnsworth insisted.

Diego stiffened but turned his ear.

"He's the only one who's seen Gage Houdek's face and I'm certain Casey Kubri—Casey Sheen won't go anywhere without him." He checked his timepiece. "He's gotta be setting up for the show with Wil Wheaton right now—we've maybe got a tiny window—it'll be harder to convince them we're the real deal if we leave Henry behind."

Setting his jaw, but relenting with a nod, Diego followed Farnsworth to the kitchen.

A few seconds later they popped the latch on the broken deep freezer. A wave of sweaty air and nervous energy rolled out as they opened the door.

Henry Sheen sat in the middle of the unit, duct taped to a chair. Blood splatters and sticky, crimson pools indicated

Houdek had worked him over something awful. He flinched as they opened the entry but relaxed when he saw it wasn't the killer returning to torture him.

"Help! You've gotta help me. I've been kidnapped and…" he finally recognized Rick Diego and his face fell again. He began babbling, trying to string together some kind of story about the mob being behind everything. "They're framing me," he insisted, "even killed your partner to make it look like I did it, yeah. McCloud was onto them—and now they're trying to kill my… friend, Casey Kubrick."

Diego fixed him with hard eyes. "Shut it. I already know everything." He spun the chair and pointed to the fan. "There's an access panel behind there. We heard you confess everything to Houdek. Now tell me why we ought to go save your brother's life?"

"My brother will be fine. Zmei said he'll spare him if he gives back the money."

"He was lying," Farnsworth said. "*Everyone* connected to this thing is getting a butterfly knife. As soon as he gives the money back, Casey is a dead man."

Henry blanched as whatever blood remained in his face drained. Tears welled up in his eyes, he'd known it in the pit of his gut, but he needed some kind of hope to cling to.

"I'll confess. I'll tell them everything if you keep us alive. *Both of us.*"

"You'll take down the Bratva, too?" Farnsworth slipped in. "Testify like you should have done a decade ago?"

He hung his head in heavy agreement.

"Yes," he sighed. "But it was only me who killed Detective McCloud."

Diego smashed a fist through his face, rattling Sheen's jaw enough to knock a tooth free. "I'm done with you lying to me, Henry! Now look me in the eyes and tell me who killed that innocent man—my friend."

Henry looked up. "I… I… my brother did it. He was so angry. Casey blamed him for arresting me all those years ago. 'It's just icing on the cake,' he said… he figured McCloud would be at the crime scene after we robbed the Bratva and so he set the trap. I... I told him it was a bad idea."

"This whole thing is wrapped in bad ideas," Diego muttered, but he tore the criminal's bonds free and slapped him in handcuffs. "Now let's go. We're gonna get your idiot brother so we can take down the Brotherhood and save a bunch of innocent lives."

The detective poked the bloody man in the back with his gun. "Now let's go—we have to hurry."

Farnsworth whipped out his phone and fired off a text. They were going to need all the help they could get.

Insert into Base

Jennifer Quast

Post pics of your weirdest scenes to
#50ShadesofWorf

50 Shades of Worf

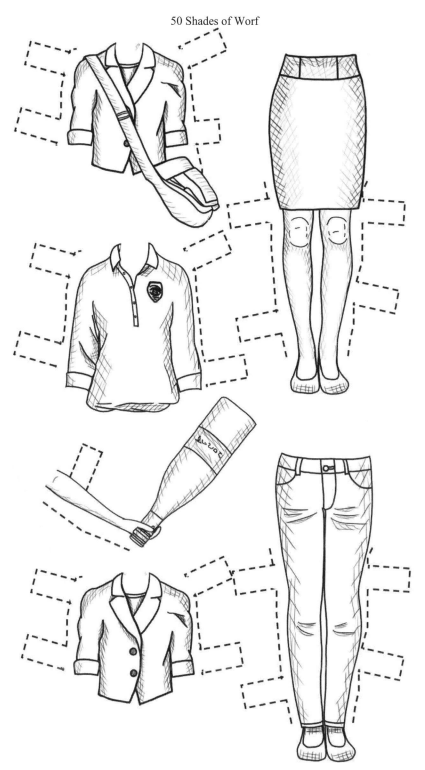

229

Post pics of your weirdest scenes to
#50ShadesofWorf

# PART SEVEN

## CLIMAX

# 63

Harley Quinn's Filibuster

Jessica followed the Confather and his security team through the clustered crowds that packed out the largest meeting hall. Without the security waving their badges as if they meant something, they would've never gotten through.

Everywhere they turned, people wore *Knights of the Illuvian Age* promo t-shirts or security uniforms. Tudyk had called in anyone he could spare leaving only a skeleton crew to mind the rest of the convention.

The front quarter of the room had been reserved for the higher dollar Kickfunder donors where space was easier to come by. Only those VIPs were able to pass the screen of security workers checking and cross-checking IDs against the donors list. Tudyk approached the line when a young man with a clipboard stopped him and Jessica.

"She's with me," Tudyk told him.

Clipboard boy held him up. "Names?"

Tudyk shot him a glare which failed to get the point across. "Do you have any idea who I am?"

The pencil pusher swallowed. "Um... you're from that TV show, right? Big Bang Theory or something like that? You still need to be on the list."

Tudyk blew a hot blast of air from his nostrils. One of the other security guards whispered into the kid's ear. He turned white and stepped aside.

They got to the front of the room and stood off to the side of the stage. A heavy drape blocked the view. It would open as soon as the panel began.

A very disinterested Michael Dorn stood at the front holding the bat'leth that they would give away to one winner during the panel. He stood on stage waiting for the event to begin once the curtains opened.

Jessica blushed as she looked Dorn up and down with hungry eyes. He stood only a few feet away. Her cell phone buzzed with a message from Farnsworth. One word: *stall*.

She unzipped the front of her tight Harley Quinn catsuit to expose more milky, white real estate. "Hey mister Dorn!" she shouted and began fangirling.

Dorn put up a hand to calm her. "I'm happily married," he said up front.

She kept going anyways, babbling about anything she could think of in order to try and filibuster the *Knights of the Illuvian Age* panel.

"Alan," he greeted the Confather calmly.

"Michael."

"Is she with you?"

Jessica prattled over their voices like white noise.

Tudyk shrugged and unrolled the artwork she'd delivered. "Kind of. Maybe. I'm not really sure at the moment."

"Hey," she interjected. "I'm significant to the plot!"

Tudyk scanned the artwork, hoping for some kind of guidance. He looked up. Furries lined the edge of the room on one side. Bronies stood opposite them with well over a thousand people in between them.

*"If this thing erupts, it's going to be total anarchy,"* he whispered to himself before turning his eyes back to the oddly erotic piece of artwork.

# 64

The Resurrection of Michael Clarke Duncan

Farnsworth and Diego worked the hallways with guns drawn. They dragged the manacled Henry Sheen with them until they arrived at the back entrance. The big detective pointed to the black marks he'd made on the door the previous day.

"This is it. I'm sure of it."

Diego pushed Sheen through the door and urged him forward.

The lights were low, ready for some theatrical presentation they'd planned for the *Knights of the Illuvian Age* event. Props, costumes, and prototype set design pieces made a sort of maze in the shadows; they had to navigate it in the dark.

They followed the voices and walked towards the lit area of stage near the colossal curtains. Casey sat adjacent to Wil Wheaton in a matching chair, ready to push the button that would draw back the curtains and begin the event. A buzzing lull of the audience barely made it past the thick fabric.

"...I can still change the casting," Casey said. "I don't have to give him the role if he keeps acting like such a tool, you know."

"Hey!" Wheaton snapped. "You don't get to say that. He's... I don't know. He's an okay guy. We're just having a little disagreement over our cats..."

Diego pushed Sheen forward into the light.

The director interrupted Wheaton and leapt to his feet. "Henry! What are you doing here? You can't be here—especially not now."

Henry stood there, banged up and bleeding. "Casey. It's gone too far... we gotta shut this down."

Wheaton looked at Casey and stood. His body language indicated he thought it best to step away from what sounded like a private conversation.

Casey put up a hand to stay him. "Henry, you've got to get out of here."

"I'm sorry," Henry's voice cracked. "We can't do this. We've got to give it all back."

"What are you talking about, Henry? We're so close... we've got all the cash we need. And just look at all the support—the people want us to make this movie."

Henry cocked his head and squinted with confusion. "We were never going to make the movie, Casey. 'Take the money and run,' that was the plan all along."

"But we can make this movie. It's happening—we've got the money, we've got the demand and the support. The cast is coming together. We're gonna make so much more off the movie... this is our chance for greatness. *I can do this* Henry! I can... Henry, why are your hands behind your back?"

"They're onto us," he insisted. "The Bratva. If we don't get out of here right now they're *gonna kill us.*"

Wheaton interjected, "Hey, guys, I don't think I want to be a part of whatever you've got going..."

"Shut up!" Casey snapped. "Henry. *Your hands?*"

Diego pushed him forward and Farnsworth brought up their flank as they walked further into the light.

Casey yanked a hand gun from beneath his shirt and pointed it at Diego. "You!"

"Whoa!" said Wheaton. He put his hands in the air and took a step back.

Casey swung his gun towards the actor. "Stay put. Nobody's going anywhere."

Diego's eyes shrank to slits as he glared down the sights of his barrel at his partner's murderer and he accused the director. "I'm guessing you first laid eyes on me from the other side of a video camera, right after you crushed my best friend."

The phony director sneered and kept his gun trained on the bearded actor who didn't dare take another step back, though he desperately wanted to. "Detective McCloud had it coming," Casey ranted. "He destroyed my family—ruined my brother's life. My parents died when I was still in high school… while my big brother was doing time in prison. They stuck me in the middle of nowhere and abandoned me! No connections. Not even a name and history to go back on after being tossed into witness protection and moved across the country. No! *You… you* are the bad guys."

He fixed Diego with eyes that burned like orbs of pure malice. "I was so glad that it was *him* who came to investigate after we took down those mob goons. Not only was I able to hurt the mob, but I got my revenge on the guy who put my brother away."

"And why the yellow spray paint?" Farnsworth asked.

"If you're going to crush someone, you might as well do it theatrically."

"Wait," Wheaton asked. "You killed a cop like the Grinning Man from the *Caped Defenders* thirty-eight variant? That's just plain sinister."

Diego's aim didn't waver as he took a hesitant step forwards.

Casey's waggling aim kept true on Wheaton who tensed as the detective advanced.

"You killed him. McCloud was my best friend… my only true friend."

"Um, what about me?" Farnsworth complained.

He didn't pay him any attention. "I don't really even care if you pull that trigger. You can shoot us all, but I'm taking you down with me."

"Does he really mean that?" Wheaton asked Farnsworth.

The junior detective did his best poker face and went all in with an unsuited two and seven.

"Casey," Henry insisted, "It's the only way. Bratva has a hit man after us. He's here already... somewhere. They want their money back—and then they're going to kill us and everyone who's affiliated in any way with the whole thing."

Wheaton piped up. "When you mean *everyone...*"

Casey stepped closer and put the gun to Wheaton's head and used him as a shield. "I guess I'll have to improvise. I'll shoot the golden boy if you don't let me out of here."

Diego shrugged. "I barely know who he is, even. Shoot him... see what happens."

"Hey!" Both Farnsworth and Wheaton yelled in unison.

"Come on, Henry," the younger brother barked. "We're getting out of here, through the crowd if we have to."

With a sheepish look on his face, Henry took a step towards his brother.

Diego grabbed him from behind and put his own pistol to the convict's head. "It looks like we're even, now. We each have someone the other side wants."

Casey's face scrunched up with rage and he dug the barrel of his gun into Wheaton's temple. "No, no, no! Put your guns down and let him go. We're getting out of here and you're not going to follow us or, I swear, I'll kill Wil Wheaton!"

Before either side could act, a shadowy figure hidden behind a cluster of stage props spoke up. His voice, low like gravel, filled the stage. "I'd rather do this up close and personal, but I'll spray and pray if I have to. I'll mow down everyone here and on the other side of that curtain."

"That voice," Wheaton said reverently, "But I thought Michael Clarke Duncan is dead..."

"Gage Houdek... Zmei... the assassin who never misses," Farnsworth whispered.

"Guns on the floor," the shadowy figure said. He began to take shape in the dark. "If anyone here is going kill Wil Wheaton, it's going to be me."

# 65

Fulcrum

A nervous energy had taken over the crowd on the public side of the curtain. The clock had turned several minutes past the hour and the panel should have already started already.

Ripples of confused conversation rose and ebbed.

The Confather studied the unrolled image. Tudyk's feverish search for answers felt futile: it was just a stupid picture. As far as he could tell, there were no mystical properties to it.

He scanned the crowd while Jessica continued prattling in his ear. The furries and bronies were on edge, ready to snap at any moment. Leaders of both factions had, for some reason, also taken out their own copies of the pegasus art print they'd acquired on the first day.

"You know, in case you're trying to stall for time," Tudyk fired over his shoulder, "you're not actually helping. The curtains are opened from the inside. Michael Dorn has no control over it."

Flabbergasted, Jessica finally shut up.

Tudyk turned his attention back to the battle-ready warriors in fluffy tails and ears. Perhaps their examination of the art meant that they didn't really want this war? If they were also searching for nonviolent solutions in the eleventh hour maybe it indicated they could still talk this through?

The murmurs of impatience flowing through the crowd seemed to reach a peak. Michael Dorn walked to the middle of the stage, holding his bat'leth.

All eyes in the room followed him. The discontent quelled as they latched onto the hope that the show would soon begin.

Dorn planted his feet and stood there at attention for a few moments. He looked behind him at the closed curtain, and then at his wrist where he might've worn a watch twenty years ago. He addressed the crowd with a shrug and an awkward, straight lipped smile.

Something like a nervous laugh of anticipation pulsed through the audience as the actor did his best to communicate that some kind of technical difficulties held up the program.

Nearly five minutes passed in tense silence before the disaffection returned.

Ever the showman, Dorn used his hands to try and dispel the rising malcontent. He hadn't been given a microphone and so he had to improvise.

The actor began spinning his bat'leth in practiced, precise moves that he'd trained for through hundreds of episodes and multiple films. He curled, twirled, and swung his weapon through deadly attack and defense moves like a martial artist demonstrating forms. Dorn, the master of Klingon moQbara' held their attention rapt with the impromptu display of alien prowess.

Tudyk grimaced as the war brewed ever nearer its boiling point. The actor may have bought him a few more minutes, but inspirational combat maneuvers from a fictional race of warriors who lived for battle might not have been his go-to choice in any given circumstance. Then again, this was comic con.

# 66

Kobayashi Maru

Gage Houdek peeled off the shroud he wore, the black cloak of a costume he'd stolen from some random cosplayer, complete with a VIP entrance badge. He grinned as if he recognized the great irony in dressing like Death.

"I know, right? Exactly like Michael Clarke Duncan," Farnsworth commented as he lowered his gun to the ground, following his partner's lead. "I thought the same thing when I first heard him."

All but Casey laid their guns down.

Houdek pointed the gun at Wheaton, first.

"You nerds are so stupid," he spat. "I'm going to enjoy killing you all, right here in geek Mecca." With his free hand he pulled out a butterfly knife and flipped it open.

"But what about the money?" Casey blurted out.

Zmei shrugged. "What about it? This has gone way past cash, now. It's about blood and pride. Besides, we've got other ways of recouping lost assets. It's not like the Bratva are a bunch of backwoods hillbillies... they have people competent with technology. They'll be able to get some of their lost money back—even though it's pennies on the dollar after what *you* cost them." He pointed his knife at Casey and grinned wickedly.

Still using Wheaton as his human shield, Casey pointed his gun squarely at the assassin's body as the killer stepped closer one foot at a time. "That's far enough! I don't care about any of those people behind me. Now you let me go or I'll shoot you in the face."

"Fool. I don't think you know much about guns." Houdek took another step to test him.

Casey jammed the gun forward and pulled the trigger on his semiautomatic handgun. Nothing, not even a click.

"Safety," the thief muttered as Houdek took another step.

He clicked the safety button and tried again. Nothing.

Another step forwards. "You've seen me before," he smirked. "I am Death."

Casey racked the slide frantically and brought the gun to bear as if living out some epic moment. "Actually, *that's a Nazgûl robe*, you idiot." He aimed and pulled the trigger.

*Click.* Casey turned whiter than Edward Cullen at a KKK convention, still clutching the useless weapon within his ham-fists.

Houdek shook his head. "You need bullets, you moron." He took out the magazine he'd earlier stolen from the distracted Goblin Hole owner. Zmei dropped the bullets to the floor as Casey checked the empty slot in his weapon's hand grip.

"I always finish what I start," Houdek growled as he pointed at the cluster of targets with the detectives flanking on either side. "I'm going to kill you, put on this nast-ghoul costume, and walk right through that crowd to escape."

Diego tried to hedge to one side and shifted away. The muscular detective obviously posed the biggest threat to Zmei and suddenly gained the killer's full attention as he moved.

Houdek shifted his position slightly and wiggled the muzzle of his weapon at the bulky Diego. "Ah, ah, ah. Get back in line. You're not going anywhere."

"Actually, it's pronounced 'Nazgûl,' or you can just call it a ring-wraith," Casey corrected the killer's inflection.

Zmei cocked his head and turned his gaze back to Casey. "And that's why you'll go first!" He aimed at the director and was suddenly flung to the ground as Farnsworth spring-tackled him from the blind spot on the edge of Houdek's vision.

As they collided, Houdek's gun fired a single shot that whizzed past the hostages' heads before the weapon clattered to the floor. The impact sent both brawlers sprawling upon the ground.

Farnsworth tumbled across the stage screaming. A butterfly knife had lodged deep in his shoulder. He landed in a heap upon the curtain controls, forcing the shroud open and flinging it wide on electric servos.

The crowd gasped as the assassin scrambled for the nearest handgun lying on the floor. Houdek snapped and fired at the closest target: Wil Wheaton.

Diego lunged forward just in time, leaping in front of the celebrity and taking a bullet in his rippling, bare chest.

The assassin took aim for a second shot just as Michael Dorn whirled around like some kind of Klingon ninja. His eyes widened and he brought his bat'leth to bear, howling like an enraged Worf. The very real sci-fi weapon hacked off the killer's gun hand before Dorn delivered a sweeping kick as part of the moQbara' maneuver. With a thud, the sometimes-Klingon planted the would-be murderer on his back.

Houdek screamed. Blood splashed across the front three rows of the crowd, coating Police Chief Cooper in red spray and ruining his Star Trek TNG costume. Right next to him, Jessica screamed and shielded herself from the gory mist.

The crowd screamed. Anarchy erupted between the rows of seating. The scent of blood was in the wind; Tudyk gasped as the furries and bronies howled their battle cries.

"Friendship magic! For Equestria!"

"Woof! Rawr! Yip!"

A very relieved Wheaton jumped into an embrace with Dorn. "Oh my God, that was close—you saved my life... *again!*"

Dorn squeezed his friend tight. "You know I can't quit you."

"Listen, I'm sorry about everything. Sometimes I get carried away... you should come by sometime and see Princess McMittens' kittens."

"I'd like that very much."

Houdek rose to his knees, keeping pressure on his stump-hand to keep from bleeding out at the opened artery. He shook his gun free from the severed appendage and aimed it at Wheaton and Dorn.

The crowd gasped as the villain took aim. Zmei screamed "Shut up..."

Jessica interrupted him, flying onstage in a sudden burst of rapid movement. She swung her over-sized hammer down and smashed Houdek with it, cold-cocking him. "There you guys are," she exclaimed to the two detectives.

Jessica dropped the mallet next to the assassin and sank to her knees. She cradled Diego against her legs and applied pressure to his wound. "Somebody call an ambulance!" she screamed.

None in the audience heard her. The anarchy in the crowd only increased as the furries and bronies closed in on each other.

Farnsworth sat up and stood, rushing to center stage. He yanked the knife from his shoulder with a yelp as he examined his partner whose wounds were tended by his friend. The assassin had been rendered unconscious and disarmed... literally.

The detective whirled around with his damaged, prosthetic tail swishing and Deadpool's tiny, cardboard wings flapping. His eyes widened as he spotted the madness in the crowd. Few of them understood what had happened on stage and they were too afraid of the swelling riot to give it much thought.

Everywhere across the conference hall the battling cosplayers suddenly skidded to a halt at the sight of the purple-skinned pegasus-man.

Farnsworth dropped the knife from his hand. As soon as he did, bronies and furries everywhere dropped to their knees and bowed before him.

"The prophecy! The prophecy!" they yelled as if Farnsworth was some kind of Aztec god or golden robot of Endor. They began to chant like ewoks.

Chief Cooper stood to his feet and clapped. First he applauded alone, and then everyone across the room began to cheer for the insanity that had just played out before them.

The police backup that Diego had earlier called for had finally broken through the religious protesters outside and gained access to the convention grounds. Red and blue lights flashed everywhere as the crowd finally began to break apart. Furries and bronies embraced. Cats and dogs lived together. It was mass hysteria, but in a good way.

# 67

Aftermath

Paramedics carrying medical kits walked up the escalators as the moving stairs carried traffic.

"Hey!" the security teams yelled at them. "No walking. Hands on the rail." They barked orders as if the emergency personnel actually had to listen to them. They merely rolled their eyes and ignored the oblivious folks with plastic badges.

At the main level, first responders loaded Diego onto a gurney. The medics checked him over and confirmed that the bullet missed anything vital as they got him ready for transport. He'd regained consciousness and seemed in good spirits even if Jessica refused to leave his side. The pain drugs helped induce a big grin on the tough-as-nails detective.

Farnsworth sat on a nearby stool where the EMTs patched up his knife wound.

Fuzzy warmth from the pain meds made Detective Diego's head swim. He called to his partner. "Hey. You did good back there. Be proud of that."

Farnsworth nodded and winced as they started stitching him up.

"I think McCloud would be proud of you too."

Farnsworth smiled. "Thank you."

The doors opened and Captain Murphy walked in with Jennifer Quast trailing right after. "Good lord," she moaned. "You guys sure made a mess out of this whole thing."

Woozy from the laceration, Farnsworth stood to greet her when Quast leaned in for a hug. He sucked in a pained gasp of air as she collided against the stab wound but didn't recoil.

"Hey!" security yelled at Quast. "No glomping!"

"We got em," Diego said in a drunken slur. "We got McCloud's killers. And I learned about comic books and movies."

"Uh huh," Murphy said, less impressed than the detectives had hoped. "Well, at least you guys *did* catch a high profile assassin, and Henry Sheen is cooperating. It sounds like they're gonna be able to go after all of the high ranking members of Bratva with his testimony."

"I think cat ears on a woman are sexy," Diego interrupted. The drugs had obviously broken his internal filter.

"Meow," Jessica teased and licked his hand. A nearby paramedic cringed.

"Yeah… Let's get him out of here before he says something he's gonna regret," the Captain ordered.

The ambulance crew began wheeling Diego out and the groggy detective shot his partner a big thumbs up like he was a kid again.

Jessica held up her hands and imitated paws. She flashed him a pouty wave as they pushed him away.

Diego called out to Farnsworth, "Let's do this again next year. But without me getting shot."

# PART EIGHT

## SEASON FINALE

# 68

McCrumb's Naughty Unicorn Bits

Moses Farnsworth knocked on the apartment door. After several long seconds the security chain scraped on the other side and the entry opened but only a crack. Rick Diego's huge form blocked the opening.

He was bare-chested. His bullet wound had mostly healed in the last two and a half weeks. It had puckered and blushed with new, pink flesh. One arm rested on the door frame, the other held something behind his back.

"Hey Rick," Farnsworth said. "I was just on my way to... somewhere, and I got a call from Captain Murphy. I wanted to let you know right away that I officially made detective. The promotion is a real thing, now."

"Great. Good job." He kept glancing over his shoulder as Farnsworth spoke. "We'll have to do something special tomorrow to celebrate or something."

Farnsworth looked at him suspiciously. "Is there something happening inside?" he murmured in case his partner was in any kind of trouble.

"Nope. Nothing weird happening here." The pitch of his voice had elevated just slightly.

"Then what are you holding behind your back?"

"This? Oh it's nothing," Diego said, but refused to show him.

Farnsworth put a toe in the door and reached for his arm. "Come on. Show it to me. What is it?"

Diego resisted, but he was still weak on that side from the recent gunshot.

Farnsworth succeeded in pulling his arm free. He grudgingly held up the copy of Sharyn J.R.R.K. McCrumb's *Knights of the Illuvian Age* that Farnsworth had given him at the convention.

"Ha! I knew you'd like it," Farnsworth said.

"I was just moving it."

"Then why is your finger holding your place between pages?" He stuck a thumb in the gap and wrested the book away. "And you're right at the crazy, erotic unicorn scene, too! It's about to get *so good.*"

Diego shot him a look that Farnsworth couldn't quite interpret. "You have no idea."

"Okay. Well. I'll leave you to it." He paused. "I'm actually on my way to pick up a date. I asked Quast out. That's not going to make anything awkward, is it?"

"Good luck. And if it *is awkward* you'll be fine. Just own it. You're already kind of awkward; but you make it work for you."

Something made noise behind Diego and Farnsworth cocked his head.

"I've kinda got a date over, myself," he said, trying to shoo his partner away.

Farnsworth scanned his eyes up and down at his shirtless partner whose dating experiences obviously surpassed his own.

"She isn't like the usual girls I go after. I kind of like this girl, too, sooooo…"

"Right." Farnsworth started to extricate himself from the threshold when Jessica opened the door further.

"Oh, hey, Moses," she said. Jessica slapped Diego on the rump. "I figured you were all kinds of repressed and into weird stuff, Rick, but I'm not sure whatever you're lining up out here is something that I'm into."

"No!" Farnsworth put up his hands and stepped backwards as nervous as a long-tail cat in a room full of rocking chairs.

"I'm not... we're not, I mean... that ship sailed... *and besides, all three of us?*"

"I'm just kidding, tiger," Jessica laughed. "I'm totally in. Moses can wear the kitten ears. I'll get my whip."

Neither of them could quite string a pair of words together. Both babbled, blushing with denials.

Jessica took the book back, careful to keep her finger in the page, and attached a unicorn horn around Diego's head with an elastic band. She slapped him again on the rear with a wink and walked back into the apartment. "Whatever. Don't take too long or I'll start without you."

Diego's cheeks and neck flushed red. Neither man could look at each other.

"So I'll just, ah, go then?" Farnsworth turned, stiff like a robot.

"Yeah... I'll see you tomorrow... partner."

Just before the door clicked shut Diego called back down the hallway. "Hey, catch." Diego tossed a ceramic plate down the corridor. "I owed you one."

Farnsworth bobbled it mid-air, but caught it and turned it over in his hands. It was the same print as the one he'd broken a few weeks ago. "I don't really need the full set. Tell your mom I said hi." He winked briefly. "I even tried a snicker-doodle. Not bad... but don't tell anyone back at the precinct about any of this or I'll kill you!"

Smiling, Farnsworth chuckled underneath his breath and wandered back down the hallway. He replied mainly for his own benefit, "Don't worry. Not a word... partner."

The End.

**NEW ACHIEVEMENT UNLOCKED!**
https://amzn.to/2Sg32Tx
[LEAVE A REVIEW FOR +2500XP]

# *Halp!*

Thank you for reading my book! I hope it made you laugh.

Would you please take a moment to leave me a review online? Amazon, Goodreads, or anyplace else you use is an awesome start. You can also share this title with your friends on social media and requesting it via your local library will also help. According to the Internet, Bill Gates is giving everyone who shares this and reviews the book 5318008 dollars! Sounds like a hoax you say? If you don't a human centipede will get you, and these things are long enough.

But seriously, reviews and recommendations help more than anything else out there. And as always, check me out online at: www.AuthorChristopherDSchmitz.com.


Thanks for reading and sharing!

Christopher D Schmitz

# SPECIAL OFFER:

Thank you so much for checking out my book! As a special bonus for you, I'd like to invite you download FIVE ebooks for free as a part of my Starter Library.

To get your free Starter Library, simply visit this link:
http://www.subscribepage.com/p1o9c9
Enter your email address and then collect your books as they are sent to you. It's that simple and you'll get the first one right away!

FREE STARTER BOOK LIBRARY

## About the author:

Christopher D. Schmitz is author of both Sci-Fi/Fantasy Fiction and Nonfiction books and has been published in both traditional and independent outlets. If you've looked into indie writers of the upper midwest you may have heard his name whispered in dark alleys with an equal mix of respect and disdain. He has been featured on television broadcasts, podcasts, and runs a blog for indie authors... but you've still probably never heard of him.

As an avid consumer of comic books, movies, cartoons, and books (especially sci-fi and fantasy) this child of the 80s basically lived out Stranger Things, but shadowy government agencies won't let him say more than that. He lives in rural Minnesota with his family where he drinks unsafe amounts of coffee; the caffeine shakes keeps the cold from killing them. In his off-time he plays haunted bagpipes in places of low repute, but that's a story for another time.

Schmitz also holds a meaningless Master's Degree and freelances for local newspapers. He is available for speaking engagements, interviews, etc. via the contact form and links on his website or via social media.

## Discover Fiction Titles by Christopher D Schmitz

The Last Black Eye of Antigo Vale
Burning the God of Thunder
Piano of the Damned
Shadows of a Superhero
The TGSPGoSSP 2-Part Trilogy
Father of the Esurient Child
Bridge of Se7en
One Star
Grandma Ethel's Donuts and Hollow Points
Dekker's Dozen: A Waxing Arbolean Moon
Dekker's Dozen: Weeds of Eden
Dekker's Dozen: Spawn of Ganymede
Dekker's Dozen: The Seed Child of Sippar Sulcus
Dekker's Dozen: The Armageddon Seeds
Dekker's Dozen: The Last Watchmen
Dekker's Dozen: Austicon's lockbox
Wolf of the Tesseract
Wolves of the Tesseract: Taking of the Prime
Wolves of the Tesseract: Through the Darque Gates of Koth
Wolves of the Tesseract: The Architect King
The Kakos Realm: Grinden Proselyte
The Kakos Realm: Rise of the Dragon Impervious
The Kakos Realm: Death Upon the Fields of Splendor
The Kakos Realm: Alpha Collection
Anthologies No.1
Anthologies No.2
The Indie Author's Bible
The Indie Author's Bible Workbook

**Please Visit**
**http://www.authorchristopherdschmitz.com**
*Sign-up on the mailing list for exclusives and extras*

**other ways to connect with me:**
Follow me on Twitter:  https://twitter.com/cylonbagpiper

Follow me on Goodreads:
www.goodreads.com/author/show/129258.Christopher_Schmitz

Like/Friend me on Facebook:
https://www.facebook.com/authorchristopherdschmitz

Subscribe to my blog:
https://authorchristopherdschmitz.wordpress.com

Favorite me at Smashwords:
www.smashwords.com/profile/view/authorchristopherdschmitz

My Amazon Author Profile:
https://amazon.com/author/christopherdschmitz

Need more paperdolls so you can finally lord over them like some kind of giant, 3 dimensional king?

You can get a printable copy of all the paperdolls at the following website:

# https://bit.ly/2pu9FFl

(But be careful, their edges deal 1d1 slashing damage and they might rise up against you if you prove to be some kind of capricious and callous paperdoll over-lord. Print them in small quantities, just in case, and don't feed them after midnight.)